Decaf Cappuccino &

M000118796

by

Sara Bourgeois

Chapter 1

Kari

It was fall in Mills Township, and hands down, one of Kari Sweet's favorite times of the year.

The farmers market just outside of town was in full swing, the leaves were turning beautiful shades of red and gold. Residents and visitors alike were flocking to the town's many hiking trails.

Of course, fall was also a great time for coffee as the first chill in the air made people think of espressos, lattés, and good old-fashioned cups of joe.

On this Saturday morning, the perfect weather was attracting more people than ever to the outdoors, and On Bitter Grounds was unusually quiet. Only a handful of customers were sitting at the shop's numerous tables.

Kari and Kasi found they were able to catch up on the internet orders and housekeeping items that had been piling up over the last few days.

"So, this is what I think we should do for our weekly special," Kasi said as Kari finished jotting down notes for a particularly large order of whole roasted coffee beans. "Cappuccino."

"Oh my gosh!" Kari said, turning to her sister with a big grin. "Guess what I was thinking for our weekly special?"

"Cappuccino?" Kasi asked innocently.

Though they acted like it, neither sister was surprised. When it came to On Bitter Grounds, they were almost always on the same page. Whether they were deciding on a new brand of flour to try, were coming up with ideas for interior remodels, or were choosing the newest special to tempt their customers' taste buds, the Sweet sisters always found they were in sync.

"You got it!" Kari confirmed. "There are just so many flavors we can do. Caramel, mocha, butterscotch, peppermint…" she trailed off as her mind wandered to the smells that would be coming out of their shop over the next week.

"What do you think about offering a decaf option?" Kasi asked. "We've got a lot of seniors who come in here and are trying to decrease their caffeine intake. I think they'd appreciate it if we had something they could still enjoy instead of having to always get the tea."

"I think that's a great idea," Kari told her. "I knew there was a reason I keep you around."

"That and my beautiful smile," Kasi said, giving her sister the goofiest grin she could muster. "I had one of the older gals from the retirement community in here the other day, and she was telling me how they all just took a class on hypertension. Apparently, caffeine is one of the biggest culprits."

"Let's hope that information doesn't get out," Kari replied playfully. "It could really hurt our business."

Kasi nodded and turned back to the laptop. After a minute, she said, "Hey, did you know where the name 'cappuccino' came from?"

"I don't have the foggiest."

Kari knew her sister loves finding out strange facts and sharing them with her. It was part of her sister's charm, and she had to admit she had learned tons of great tidbits from her over the years.

Kasi was the sole reason she knew that Starbucks was named after a minor Moby Dick character, and that Mocha, a city in Yemen, had been one of the centers in the early coffee trade.

"It's named after the Capuchin monks in Italy," Kasi told her. "When the drink was first introduced there, they thought the color of it matched the color of the monk's robes."

"Huh," Kari said, nodding her head. "That makes sense. Did the monks actually drink it?"

"That, I don't know. But don't you think it would be cool if we could incorporate that history into our sign this week? Maybe you could call Rebecca Trang, and ask her if she knows how to draw a monk sipping a hot drink?"

Rebecca was a local artist the girls had known for years, and who they had recently hired to draw their weekly chalk signs, which stood outside the front doors of the shop. Not only was Rebecca an incredibly talented artist, but she was also from Mills Township, and the girls always loved a chance to support a fellow local businesswoman.

Rebecca's artwork had appeared in galleries up and down the coast, and she has a big show coming up in Boston at the end of the month. They'd been lucky that she'd agreed to work for them in between her larger projects.

"I'll give her a call right now," Kari confirmed, grabbing her cell phone and finding Rebecca on her contact list.

When she answered, Kari told her a little bit about what they were thinking for the sign that week.

"She thinks it's a great idea!" she told her sister when they hung up. "She even has an idea about making the monk a Capuchin monkey! Wouldn't that be cute?"

"Perfect!" Kasi said with a smile.

"Should we do walnut bread, too? I found a great new recipe on the internet last week. It's got a touch of cinnamon and brown sugar and should go well with all the distinct types of flavors. Do monkeys like walnuts? We could have our monkey monk eating some bread, too!"

Kari shook her head and giggled. "This is getting a little silly. But I do think walnut bread is the perfect choice."

The two girls chatted happily about how much their customers would enjoy the special as they finished up their internet orders and put together a stack of boxes for the mailman to pick up on his daily route.

"Do you realize that our online orders are starting to bring in more money than what we sell in the shop?" Kasi asked as she went through the billing invoices for what they had just shipped out.

"I know it had to be getting close," Kari said, looking over her shoulder at the laptop.

"Do you think that's a good thing or a bad thing?"

Kari shrugged. "Neither. I think if we have two strong revenue incomes, it's a solid business model. That way, if either of them takes a dive, we can still rely on the other."

"That makes sense," Kasi said. "I guess I'm just kind of sad that we don't ever get to talk to these people we send coffee to. I love making friends with our customers and learning about their lives. It's one of my favorite parts of this job."

"Me too," Kari agreed. "But I also like knowing that our coffee is being shipped all over the United States. Can you imagine? There are people right now in Alaska brewing On Bitter Grounds in their homes."

"You mean in their igloos?" Kasi said with a laugh. "Yeah, that's a pretty fun thought."

When the phone rang a couple of hours later, the sisters had just pulled their first test loaf of the weekly special out of the oven.

"Oh my, smell this!" Kasi said, shoving the pan under Kari's nose. "I think I want to eat the whole thing right now."

Kari nudged her away so she could answer the phone. It was Rebecca, telling her the sign was ready.

"Is she going to deliver it?" Kasi asked.

"No, I told her I'd go pick it up," Kari answered, reaching for her jacket. "She lives in The Abbey, and I haven't had a chance to see it yet, so I thought it would be a fun little field trip."

"Cool, I'll man the shop while you're gone. I can't wait to see it, I bet she did a fantastic job!"

Kari zipped up her jacket and wondered if she should also put on her scarf. Though she loved fall, she was not a huge fan of the cold winds that could sometimes take you by surprise. As someone who had lived on the coast her entire life, she'd have thought she'd be used to it by now, but the changing of the season always left her a little chilled.

Deciding to forego the scarf, she hurried to the door and saw a blue Silverado pull up outside.

"Oooooh, looks like your boyfriend is here!" Kasi trilled from behind the counter. "Sure, you don't want Rebecca to drop off the sign, so you can do a little flirting?"

Kari sent her sister a glare over her shoulder.

"I'm sure you can get Mr. Officer his coffee order, this time."

She watched as Hunter, in all his blond perfection, step out of his truck.

Well, this day just got a little better, she thought. AND a little bit more exciting. Hunter always made the butterflies in her stomach go crazy.

Chapter 2

Hunter

It was Hunter's Saturday off, but he was headed in to work to cover for a co-worker for a few hours, so that he could attend his son's basketball game.

Mills Township was a relatively small town, but they took their youth sports programs very seriously.

Before he went in, Hunter decided that he was going to swing by and grab a bite to eat at On Bitter Grounds.

If everything went according to plan, he would have a date with Kari Sweet that very evening.

Just as he pulled up in front of the coffee shop, Hunter noticed Kari heading out the door.

Just my luck, he thought. *She's on her way out.*

Before she had gotten too far down the sidewalk, Hunter quickly jumped out of his truck and greeted her.

"Hey, Kari. Where are you headed in the middle of the day? Don't tell me that you're running off and letting your little sister do all the work."

Hunter loved to tease the beautiful woman who stood before him.

Kari playfully punched Hunter's arm and said, "You know me better than that! I'm going to The Abbey to pick up our new sign board for the sidewalk from Rebecca Trang."

"Rebecca Trang. I don't think I know her, but I have noticed your signs have gotten a lot better and more colorful lately."

"We try to please not only the sense of taste and smell, but occasionally, we also like to give our customers something pretty to look at."

Hunter smiled as Kari blushed, realizing the predicament she had put herself in. "I doubt any of your customers have ever had to complain about a lack of beauty while visiting your shop."

As the crimson blush that crept across Kari's face deepened in hue, she stammered, "I didn't mean it the way it came out. I was...I was...well, I wasn't fishing for a compliment if that's the way it sounded. I just meant that to keep people's interest, we needed something fresh each week, and the signs are an eye-catching way to do that."

Hunter let out a laugh that would have had most women seethe with anger thinking they were the butt of some terrible joke. But not Kari Sweet. Almost immediately, she was giggling right along with him.

"I'm glad I amuse you, Mr. Houston." Kari grinned, knowing that Hunter felt silly every time she called him that.

"Okay, okay. I give up. You win, just please don't make me feel like my father." Hunter threw his hands up in surrender. "And to think I came here on important business!"

"Important business. This sounds serious." For a second, Kari had a worried expression on her face.

"Nothing horrible. At least, I don't think it is. I just wondered what you were doing for dinner tonight."

Sheepishly, Hunter stared at the ground like a young boy who had just asked someone out on his very first date.

"I don't have any real plans just yet." Kari answered shyly.

Hunter looked up to stare directly into Kari's eyes. For a moment, he was mesmerized by the emerald green that was staring back at him. "I wondered if you'd like to go to the diner tonight after you close the shop?"

"That sounds nice. I'd love to."

"Great! About six o'clock, is that okay?"

"That's perfect. It will give me plenty of time to close the shop and get everything ready for Monday."

"So, I'll see you at six." Hunter shifted nervously, unsure of what to say next.

"I'd better get going. Rebecca is expecting me to be there soon. I'm looking forward to seeing you later."

Frozen in place, Hunter couldn't take his eyes off her as she walked away.

Kari was not an ordinary girl, he had to admit. Not only was she beautiful and smart, but she also had an amazing personality and genuinely cared for those around her.

That was a quality that Hunter really respected.

Most of the girls Hunter had dated in the past had been too self-absorbed to worry about anything more than their profiles on Facebook and Instagram, let alone do something productive for society.

Kari, on the other hand, was different. She worked hard trying to build a small business in Mills Township and never missed an opportunity to return something positive to the community that she lived in.

Once she reached her Jeep, Kari turned and waved to Hunter, then climbed inside and drove away.

A deep grin suddenly spread across Hunter's face as he allowed his imagination to run wild for a few moments.

He pictured himself sitting across from Kari and staring into those enchanting green eyes. After they finished their dinner, he would suggest they take a short stroll around the downtown businesses and enjoy the evening air.

Since it was still a little nippy in the evenings, Kari might just get a little cold, giving Hunter the opportunity to place his arm around her shoulders. Who knows, he might even find the right moment to kiss Kari for the first time.

"I'm looking forward to seeing you tonight, too," Hunter muttered to himself as he finally turned and walked into the coffee shop.

Once he opened the door, Hunter was met by the smell of freshly brewed coffee and something sweet that he couldn't exactly identify. Quickly, he scanned the glass display case, hoping that he would be able to find the owner of the tempting smell.

Unfortunately, his attention was not completely on the task at hand. He was still distracted by thoughts of Kari.

On his third pass over the case, he suddenly became aware that someone was watching him. He glanced around the room only to see that there was no one behind him.

As he turned back to the case, he was met head on by Kasi's amused expression.

"Kasi! What are you doing?"

"I was just going to see how long it was going to take you to answer me," she replied.

"What are you talking about? You didn't ask me anything."

"Actually, I did the moment you walked in the door. Apparently, you just had your mind on something--or someone--more important."

Hunter suddenly felt his face grow hot. "I'm sorry, I guess I was preoccupied. What did you ask me?"

"I just wanted to know what, or should I say who, were you grinning about?"

Hunter felt his face deepen in color, if that was even possible, causing Kasi to burst out laughing at his expense.

"What's so funny?" Hunter stammered.

"If you don't see it yourself, you've got bigger troubles on your hands than I can help with."

"Look, Kasi, I'm not sure what you're talking about. Can you please tell me what's so funny?"

"Man, you do have it bad for my sister, don't you?"

Once again, Hunter's face burned, embarrassed that someone knew his secret. Unfortunately, that someone just had to be Kasi. It didn't matter what he said now, Kasi wasn't going to let it go easily.

"Oh, shut up!" Hunter playfully scolded her. "If you're done, I'd like to order a cup of coffee and a tuna sandwich, please. To go."

Kasi shook her head at Hunter.

"I'm not sure why you're so embarrassed. I think it's great you like my sister."

Hunter started to interrupt, but Kasi stopped him.

"I wouldn't bother to deny it, either. The evidence is all over your face every time you look at her. And, for what it's worth, I think you two would make a great couple. If anyone was to ask my opinion."

"No one has to ask," Hunter teased, "You'll just give it regardless if we ask or not."

He gave her a mischievous wink as she handed him the bag containing his sandwich. He knew she meant well, and Hunter was glad he had Kasi's seal of approval. Her opinion meant a lot to Kari, and Hunter knew he wouldn't make it far if Kasi didn't like him.

As he exited the shop, Hunter couldn't help but scold himself for reacting to Kasi's teasing, though. He knew he must have turned every shade of red.

I hope she doesn't say anything to Kari that would make her uncomfortable on our date tonight, he thought.

Hunter cranked up his truck as thoughts about his impending date entered his mind. Is it really that obvious that I'm crazy about Kari Sweet?

Turning his head slightly, he stared in the direction her Jeep had driven just a short while ago. I wonder if she has it as bad for me as I have for her? I think I just might have some detective work to do.

Suddenly, he pictured Kari's face as Kasi scandalously dished out the juicy details of how he'd acted after she left him standing on the sidewalk.

I've got to get it together.

Kari's a nice girl, but there's no way she's even going to entertain the idea of going out with me if she thinks I'm a bumbling idiot.

Chapter 3

Kari

As Kari made the short drive out to The Abbey, she couldn't help but play the scene with Hunter over and over in her mind. He seemed as nervous around her as she was around him.

Am I imagining things? She asked herself. *Or is it just wishful thinking?*

She turned up the radio on the Jeep, hoping it would drown out her thoughts.

No such luck. She just couldn't stop seeing that smile.

That man had some of most gorgeous dimples she had ever seen. The best part was, he seemed completely oblivious to how he affected every woman he came near.

Kari had seen little old ladies in the shop swoon when he turned that smile their way, but Hunter didn't even seem to notice.

She glanced in the rearview mirror and adjusted a few pieces of her curly hair. She was glad she'd put some extra effort into it this morning, instead of just throwing it up into a bun or messy ponytail like usual.

Unfortunately, the Star Wars t-shirt she was wearing was covered in flour, sugar, and a bit of frosting from the morning's baking frenzy.

"Oh well, what does he expect?" she asked herself out loud. "After all, I do work in a coffee shop."

Even so, she knew she'd have to put a little more effort into her outfit when the two of them met for dinner. She thought about swinging home after she was done picking up the sign, she could put on a fresh shirt and maybe put on a bit more makeup.

She was, thankfully, saved from her obsessive thoughts about Officer Houston when she pulled into The Abbey, a converted convent on the edge of town.

The structure had been turned into condos a few years back, and the grounds had been meticulously landscaped. Though Kari had driven by it numerous times, she'd never actually been on the property. She was excited to get a close-up look, especially since the high brick walls had prevented her from seeing much from the outside, and trespassers were strictly forbidden.

Pulling up outside the building, she got ready to check her phone for the unit number Rebecca had texted her earlier.

Before she could find it, though, she saw the artist skipping out of the front door.

"Hi!" she said, when Kari got out of her Jeep. "I saw you pull up, so thought I'd just run out to meet you."

Rebecca was in her late 30s and had long blonde hair that always swung free and which looked like it hadn't been cut in years.

Today, she was wearing bell bottom jeans and a flowing blouse, that Kari was pretty sure she'd seen in a documentary she'd watched recently about Woodstock.

Rebecca was certainly a free spirit, but Kari thought it was probably the secret behind her incredible creativity and talent.

"This place is amazing," Kari said as they walked across the grounds to the outbuilding, where Rebecca and a few other artists who lived there kept a studio.

"Aren't there some pretty wild local legends surrounding its history?"

"Oh, you bet there are!" Rebecca said brightly. "That's one of the reasons why I love this place!"

She opened the door to the building and gestured at the elevator in the corner of the landing.

"There's an elevator, but I wouldn't recommend it. It gets stuck about every other time we use it. Last time, my friend Keith was trapped in there for almost two hours."

Kari cringed. "I hope he didn't have to go to the bathroom!"

Rebecca chuckled. "You know, I never thought to ask."

"I prefer the stairs anyway," Kari assured her. "Gotta get my cardio in somehow, right?"

Rebecca laughed.

"Well, the stairs aren't much more reliable. I swear, you'd think they'd have redone the staircase when they converted all these buildings, but they must have thought keeping them as is was more historically accurate."

"All the studios are on the higher floors?" Kari asked as they entered the shadowy stairwell.

"Yep. Two on the second and two on the third. I think this building used to be where they put the naughty nuns. It's like the Tower of London!"

The two focused on the creaky stairs as they climbed, deciding they'd better keep the conversation to a minimum for safety's sake.

"Oh, wow," Kari breathed when they finally made it to the third floor, and she saw Rebecca's studio. "This is amazing!"

The space was bright and open with windows that offered a 360-degree view of the grounds.

There was a small kitchenette that had been updated with the newest granite and stainless-steel appliances, and Kari could just catch a glimpse of an adorable powder room through a half-closed door.

Everywhere she looked, there were stacked canvasses.

Though she'd known Rebecca was talented, she hadn't realized exactly how talented until she saw the incredible range of colors, styles, and subject matters in the paintings.

"My gosh, Rebecca. These are fantastic!"

"Thank you," Rebecca said with a shy smile. "I'm probably in this studio so much that I should just give up my condo and live here. Half the time, I end up washing my hair in the bathroom sink, so I don't have to go back home for a shower!"

She led Kari over to the corner where her chalkboard was located.

"What do you think? I loved the idea of a monkey in monk's robes. I hope it turned out as cute as it was in my head."

Kari thought the sign was perfect. The adorable little monkey had a friar's haircut and was holding a steaming mug in his hands, his cheeks pink from the warmth.

"Oh, Rebecca. It's more than I could have hoped for!"

"Yay!" Rebecca clapped her hands in delight. "I'm so glad you like it."

The two decided it would be tempting fate to try to drag the sign back down the stairs, so they took their chances on the elevator. Amazingly, it got them to the bottom floor with only a few groans.

"You want me to help you get that in your Jeep, and I can give you a short tour?" Rebecca asked. "This place is pretty cool."

"I'd love that!"

Kari was happy she hadn't had to suggest it herself. She was dying to see more of the old convent.

"So," Rebecca started after they'd secured the sign, "the story goes that in the 1900s, a young nun became pregnant here at The Abbey."

"Really?" Kari asked, following Rebecca as she walked toward the center of the grounds.

"Yep. And what's even more scandalous is that the father turned out to be one of the priests. Instead of facing the shame, she threw herself off the roof right about…there."

Rebecca pointed to the roof of The Abbey's main building.

"You sure she didn't just run off with her lover?" Kari asked, thinking that a joke would reduce the chill she suddenly felt creeping up her spine.

Rebecca shook her head. "They say you can still see her on the anniversary of her death. She throws herself off the roof again and disappears before she can hit the ground."

The chill got worse.

"And…that doesn't bother you? I mean, living here with a ghost?"

"No way!" Rebecca seemed surprised by the suggestion. "I love it! Unfortunately, I haven't seen her…yet! There's still hope, though. Her anniversary is coming up!"

Kari shuddered.

She couldn't imagine living somewhere with such a grim history. It seemed odd that someone with such a warm and bubbly personality would be interested in ghosts, but then Rebecca always was a bit odd.

"Thanks so much for the tour," Kari told her after they'd finished walking around the grounds, and Rebecca had shown her the spacious condo she rarely spent time in.

"It really is an...interesting place!"

"You bet! I'm just glad you like the sign. I've already gotten a few new clients from people who've seen them at your coffee shop."

"Really? That's great! Maybe we should think about putting some of your other paintings up inside?"

"I would love that!"

"I'll talk to my sister about it."

Kari thanked her one final time before jumping into her Jeep.

As she pulled out, she looked in her rearview mirror for a final look at The Abbey. *Now I see why people think it's creepy,* she thought. *I think I'd be fine if I never need to come back here again.*

***

The sisters spent the rest of the day serving customers and receiving compliments on their new sign.

"I'd say she nailed it," Kasi said as they finally turned the 'open' sign to 'closed' and started going through their closing checklist.

"Absolutely," Kari agreed. "She's so talented."

"Sooooo," Kasi said playfully as they swept the floors. "I see a new outfit hanging in the bathroom. I assume that's for your big date?"

Kari focused on her sweeping, so her sister couldn't see her blush.

"I didn't figure my sweaty, stained t-shirt would be too appropriate."

"Maybe, he likes you that way," Kasi suggested, batting her eyes. "Oh, I'm just messing with you," she added when her sister didn't answer. "I'm excited for you."

"What are you going to do for dinner?" Kari asked.

She was acutely aware of the fact that she had been abandoning her sister more and more due to her involvement with Hunter, and she couldn't help but feel a little guilty.

"I was thinking a date with a grilled cheese and some bad reality TV," Kasi answered.

"Why don't you take the Jeep in case you want to go somewhere? I'll just have Hunter drop me off when we're done."

"Oh great, I get to drive the orange beast," Kasi grumbled, then shot her sister a big smile.

"Don't stay out too late, honeybunch."

"Oh, I won't, Mom."

Kasi stuck out her tongue and leaned the broom against the wall.

"Well, that's that. Don't want to keep Prince Charming waiting."

Kari enjoyed the fall as air as she made the quick walk to the diner. She couldn't help but feel grateful for everything that was in her life despite the recent events in Mills Township.

She knew how lucky she was to work with her sister, and that neither of them had to answer to a boss or manager.

She was so caught up in her thoughts that she almost walked right by the diner.

You goofball, she chided herself as she turned to open the door.

Now's not the time to get lost in your head. It's time to enjoy an evening with Mills Township's finest.

Chapter 4

Hunter

Hunter pulled his truck into a space in front of Sally's Diner.

Quickly, he scanned the area to see if Kari had arrived ahead of him.

Good, she's not here yet. Hopefully, there's no one in the back booth, so I can snag it for us. It's nice and private back there.

Hunter smiled at the thought of spending the evening alone with Kari.

As he hurried inside, Hunter peered over the top of the seated customers to view the back booth.

A huge grin crossed his face as he saw that Kari was already seated and waiting for him. *I wonder if she had the same idea that I had?*

For a moment, Hunter couldn't move. He suddenly felt his heart in his throat. Swallowing hard, he tried to calm his nerves.

"She's stunning," he murmured to himself.

Kari wore a fitted emerald green sweater that Hunter could tell, even from this distance, perfectly matched her eyes. Her hair was draped over one shoulder in a loose braid with errant curls that framed her face.

He couldn't take his eyes off her.

"Hello, Hunter. Are you looking for someone?"

Tearing his eyes away from Kari, Hunter turned in the direction of the voice. He realized that a waitress was attempting to maneuver around him with a full tray of food. "Sorry about that," he said as he quickly sidestepped and let her pass.

As he turned once more, he saw that Kari had spotted him standing in the middle of the restaurant looking like a goon.

Smiling sheepishly, Hunter crossed the room and quickly sat down.

"Everything okay?" Kari asked a breathless Hunter.

"Yeah, everything's fine. I didn't see your Jeep outside, so when I spotted you in the corner, I was a little surprised. Where's your car?"

"Kasi rode with me to work today, so I let her take my car home. You don't mind dropping me off at my house later, do you?"

Hunter could hardly believe his luck but didn't want Kari to know just how excited he was that he was going to take her home tonight.

"Well, I don't know. It really is out of my way," Hunter teased. "Normally, I wouldn't go to all that trouble to give someone a ride, but I guess I could make an exception tonight."

"So, that's how it's going to be?" Kari wagged her finger at him. "Just for that, on the way home, you can stop and buy me an ice cream for dessert!"

Hunter laughed. "Since you put it that way, how could I refuse?"

Just then, the waitress walked up to the table.

"What can I get you both?"

They each ordered the steak special, and the waitress retreated to the kitchen.

"Well, how did your sign turn out?" Hunter asked.

"I think it's absolutely beautiful! I can't wait for you to see it. It has a monkey dressed up as a monk advertising cappuccino. Kasi came up with the idea after reading that cappuccino was named after the group of monks that invented it."

"Now that's something you don't hear every day. A group of monkeys invented coffee." Hunter winked as he teased Kari. "Seriously though, I bet its nice. I can't wait to see it."

"Have you ever been to the Abbey?" Kari asked.

"Sure, lots of times as a kid. Almost all the boys I grew up with went out there at one time or another to see if all the rumors about it being haunted were true or not. How about you? Have you gone out there before?

"Oh no, not me. I've driven by many times and wondered what was behind those walls, but until today, I'd never even peeked inside the gates."

Kari leaned in and whispered, "After the story that Rebecca told me today, I'm a little disappointed that I never went before. Did you know that the Abbey is supposed to be haunted by a ghost nun?"

"Heard it? I went every year on the anniversary hoping to get a glimpse of that old nun," Hunter said with a chuckle. "But I never saw her. My guess is that no one ever will." Hunter smiled as he watched Kari's eyes dance while talking.

"You surprise me. I never would have picked you for a ghost hunter." Kari said. "I remember hearing about the Abbey, and it being haunted as I grew up, but didn't remember hearing the nun story until today. That was always more of a Kasi thing. She's even been out there several times trying to find some ghosts. I don't really remember why I never got into stuff like that growing up. I guess I'm making up for lost time now."

"You know if you're really interested in ghost hunting, I hear that there are some really intriguing tours you can book online," Hunter told her.

"They take you to places around the country that are supposedly haunted. I even heard of one that lets you spend the night in an abandoned asylum filled with the ghosts of past guests."

The expression on Kari's face was too much for Hunter. She stared at him wide-eyed and open-mouthed.

"No thank you!" she said emphatically. "I said I thought that the story behind the Abbey is interesting, but I'm not crazy. I don't really believe in ghosts and stuff like that, anyway. Besides, I wouldn't put it past the producers of some of those shows to fake the whole thing for ratings."

Hunter chuckled, "You're probably right. I've watched a few of those shows and I must admit, it looked fake to me. But the Abbey is one of our local urban legends, so I guess it wouldn't hurt to support that one."

Just then, the waitress walked up with their orders, and the two dug into their dinners.

"How's your steak?" Hunter asked after they had each taken a bite.

"Oh, it's great. Nice and tender. How about yours?" Kari asked.

"I love their steaks. I think theirs is probably the best I've ever eaten." Hunter eyed Kari with a confused expression on his face. "I must admit, I'm glad you aren't one of those women who eat nothing but yogurt and salads all day. I always felt guilty eating like this in front of those types of girls."

Kari wondered if she should be embarrassed. She'd always had a big appetite, and it had never seemed to catch up with her.

"I suppose salads would be healthier, but I really find them boring. Not to mention the fact that it's a little hard to justify eating only a salad only at dinner, when that's your only meal. We get so busy over breakfast and lunch. Kasi and I barely have time to grab a snack some days!"

"No doubt." Hunter agreed. "I'm glad to see the business picking up for you guys."

"Thanks!" Kari was genuinely flattered that someone had taken notice of all the hard work she and Kasi were putting into the store.

"We do seem to be a little busy right now, but it might not always be that way. We must make the most of it while it lasts. That's one reason we're trying to boost our online business. It's going to help us in the long run."

"I'm glad to hear that. I hope you guys get to be in business for a really long time."

For the next few minutes, Hunter and Kari talked about each of their career paths while eating their dinner.

Just as they had finished, Hunter's phone rang. "I'm sorry, I have to take this, it's the shift supervisor calling."

"I understand." Kari said. "Don't worry about me, it might be something important."

"Thanks," Hunter mouthed as he answered the call. "Houston here...Yes sir...I understand sir...I'll head over there right now, sir."

Sighing, Hunter broke the news to Kari. "I'm afraid that I have to go out to the Abbey. There's been an accident."

"Oh, no," Kari sighed. "I hope it isn't too bad?"

"He didn't say. There's an officer on her way there as we speak. Would you like to come with me? I can drop you off when were finished."

Kari smiled. "I was hoping you'd suggest that. I'd love to come if you're sure you don't mind?"

"Of course not. I've been to your place of work plenty of times and watched you work. Tonight, you get to see me in action."

Hunter quickly paid the bill, and together they walked to his truck. As they reached the door, he opened it for her and offered her a hand getting in.

"Such a gentleman!" Kari teased.

As Hunter closed the door, he smiled to himself and thought, She's definitely into me.

Chapter 5

Kari

"So, what's going on?" Kari asked as they climbed into Hunter's truck.

Her heart was beating faster than normal, but she didn't know if it was due to the police call, or if it was just the proximity to Hunter. She had to admit, the more she was around the hunky officer, the more she liked him.

"It seems there was an accident at the Abbey," Hunter told her as he put Babe into gear and pulled into the street.

"I'm really sorry it interrupted our date. You know how police work goes. When you must be somewhere, you have to be somewhere!"

"Oh, don't worry about me," Kari assured him. "I understand. I'm just a little worried that something happened at the Abbey. I have a friend who lives there." Her thoughts immediately turned to Rebecca. *Was she okay?* Surely, it couldn't have involved her. After all, there had to be at least thirty or more residents at the old convent. "Do you know what happened?"

Hunter shook his head. "I didn't ask many questions. They just said to get out there as soon as I could."

He turned his eyes away from the road for a moment, to give Kari a reassuring smile. "I'm sure your friend is fine."

Kari nodded and tried not to worry. After all, it could be something totally innocent, and she didn't want to ruin the amazing night they were having by overthinking it.

"Maybe someone finally saw the ghost nun," she joked, trying to keep the mood light. "They could have thought it was a real person and called it in as a possible suicide!"

Hunter turned to her again with a wry smile.

"Well, let's just hope that's the case. Not just because I've always wanted to see that thing, but also because it would mean that no one got hurt. You know how local legends go. Sometimes, kids pick up on them and want to scare people by pretending they're real. It wouldn't surprise me at all if this was just some high school prank."

"That's true," Kari said, her thoughts unwillingly turning back to Rebecca. Even if it was just a prank, her friend could be scared—or even hurt.

Having a prank go horribly wrong was certainly not unheard of. She resisted the urge to send her a quick text to make sure she was okay. They'd be at the Abbey soon enough, and she'd be able to confirm her friend's health with her own eyes.

Is there really going to be another death in our town? She couldn't help but wonder as they drove.

Hunter clicked on the radio as they made the short drive to the edge of town. He seemed to want the distraction as well, though neither of them listened to the pop music that came on.

"Uh-oh," Hunter said as they pulled into the driveway for the Abbey and were met by a huge crowd of people being held back by an officer.

"That's Jo Kingston, remember? They call her in when they think things are going to get rough."

Kari looked at Jo, who appeared to be about 50 years old, and had a short silver blonde bob and stocky build. She'd seen her before, but that night had been so traumatic that most of it was a blur. Jo sometimes worked as Hunter's partner, but not often enough that Kari was super familiar with her.

"They call in a woman when they need the heavy guns?" she asked, then immediately felt anti-feminist. "I mean, I'm sure she's awesome and everything."

"Jo is an absolute firecracker," Hunter confirmed. "If there is one person on the force that you can't get anything over on, it's Jo. Can you believe she's our best bouncer when we have events? I've seen her stop a 300-pound man cold in his tracks with just a look."

Kari observed her for a few seconds with the crowd. "You know, that doesn't surprise me a bit."

He rolled down his window when Jo approached. "Jo! What happened?"

"Oh, hi, Hunter," she said when she saw him. She peered further into Babe to see who his companion was. "Kari Sweet, hello, I wish we could meet under better circumstances."

"Hi," Kari said, giving the older woman a tentative wave. "Do you know if Rebecca is okay? Rebecca Trang? She's a friend of mine and she lives here."

Jo shook her head. "I don't know much of anything other than that there is a dead body here dressed like a nun."

Kari sucked in a breath. "A real dead body?" she blurted nervously.

Jo looked at Hunter with a cocked eyebrow, as if to say, where did you pick this one up? "No, a fake dead body. We're all here to investigate a fake dead body."

41

Kari felt her face burning with embarrassment. "I didn't mean...I just...I guess I'll shut up now."

She tried to sink down in her seat as far as she could. Now, she could see why they called Jo in for the hard stuff. The woman was a bulldog.

Hunter patted her knee, which instantly made her feel better.

"You just wait here, okay?" he said to her. "I'll help get this crowd under control and try to find out where your friend is."

He hopped out of the truck and, with a booming voice, ordered the crowd to back up.

Kari leaned closer to the window to watch him work, amazed at how the crowd instantly responded to him. She saw him lean toward Jo and ask her what she knew about the dead body.

Kari leaned as close as she could, pressing her face against the window, but she couldn't hear Officer Kingston's reply.

Was someone trying to re-enact the ghost nun scenario? She wondered as she scanned the crowd for Rebecca.

Was it a prank gone horribly wrong?

As she looked at the crowd, she saw some familiar faces, though none of them, unfortunately, was Rebecca.

She identified Damon Greer, the nephew of another Abbey resident that Rebecca had told her was visiting from Portland, Oregon.

She also saw Sam and Mary Finch, more residents of the former convent who were currently being questioned by Officer Kingston. They both looked frightened, their faces drained of color.

Of course, talking to Jo could do that to a person. Kari herself now knew from experience.

Oh look, there's Penny Green! She thought when she saw the cute little blonde's familiar face.

Penny had been a good friend of Kasi's in high school and now worked at the local theater. Though she and Kari's sister hadn't really reconnected since Kasi had been back in town, she still held fond memories of the perky little actress who had starred in all the school plays.

I didn't know she was living here, too. Maybe she knows Rebecca.

Finally, with a sigh of relief, she saw Rebecca Trang, standing by herself in the crowd and looking a little lost.

Did I really think Rebecca was the body in the nun's outfit?
She asked herself, shaking her head.

Totally not possible.

But she had to admit to herself that, with the way
their luck was going, it wasn't out of the question that
the person who had died was someone they knew.

"Kari!" Rebecca spotted her through the window and
gave her a wave.

She was wearing another variation of the outfit she'd
had on when Kari picked up the sign: hip-hugging
pants with wide bottoms and a peasant blouse with a
tie-dye design. Her feet were clad in clogs that
clunked on the asphalt as she started to jog toward
the truck.

Kari opened the door and rushed over to her friend,
pulling her into a hug.

"Are you okay?" she asked. "I was so scared when I
heard something had happened at the Abbey!"

"Yes, I'm fine," Rebecca replied, pulling back and
letting out a long breath. "I don't know what's going
on, though!"

Kari put an arm around her. "Just calm down, the
professionals are here now. Just tell me what you
saw."

Chapter 6

Kari

"Oh, my goodness! Rebecca, are you okay?" Kari asked her friend as she hugged her tightly.

"I'm fine but the Nun isn't! What in the world happened?" Rebecca was visibly shaken by the scene that had unfolded on her front lawn.

"Honestly, I'm not sure. I was going to ask you the same thing. Do you know the Nun?"

As if in shock, Rebecca shook her head but could not take her eyes off the body lying on the lawn. "No one that I know is a Nun. I thought she must have been visiting someone here but everyone that I asked said that they didn't know her."

Kari looked around at the crowd hoping to see someone that recognized the woman. Unfortunately, everyone looked as clueless as she was at that moment. Turning back to Rebecca, Kari motioned toward an empty bench.

"Would you like to sit down?"

As if she were starting to overcome her initial shock, Rebecca finally looked at Kari and said, "I think I'd better." As the pair made their way through the crowd of people that had gathered, Kari couldn't help but wonder where all the people came from.

As they each took a seat, Rebecca exclaimed, "I can't believe that I actually wanted to see the "ghost run". I'd like to take that statement back, now that I've seen the results of the real-life version." Teary-eyed, she turned to Kari and said, "That poor woman. I wonder where she fell from?"

"How do you know that she fell?" Kari asked.

"That's what everyone was saying when I got down here. That she fell from somewhere in the Abbey. I can't believe this is happening!" Rebecca placed her hands over her face and just sat motionless for a few moments.

Not wanting to overwhelm her, Kari remained silent for a few minutes waiting for Rebecca to collect herself.

When she finally looked up, Kari was thankful that she seemed calm enough to talk to.

"I'm so sorry that you're having to go through this. I know how upsetting it can be to find someone dead. Is there anything I can do for you?" Kari placed her hand on that of her friend hoping to give her some amount of comfort.

"I had heard that you and Kasi had the unfortunate luck of finding a few dead bodies of your own. It must be very uncomfortable being here now and having to see another." Rebecca said.

Kari smiled weakly. *You don't know how uncomfortable it is,* she thought. But not wanting to upset her friend, she said instead, "Sadly, I think it's become less and less shocking each time we stumble upon another one. Maybe I'm just numb right now, though, from the shock."

Trying to change the subject, Kari asked, "Wow! There are a lot of people here. Do you know everyone?"

Rebecca looked around for a moment then answered. "Well, most of them I do. There are some neighbors who undoubtedly heard the sirens and came over to see what was going. The rest are residents and, of course, the cops that are milling around. But that's it. Why do you ask?"

"No reason, really. I thought that it looked like there were more people gathered here than those who live here. I guess a lot of people were just curious." Kari said. But inside she thought, *I wonder if one of these people pushed the Nun?*

For a while Rebecca and Kari sat and watched the officers question everyone that was a potential witness. As they moved through the crowd, Kari tried to catch as much of the conversations as she could. Unfortunately, she could only make out a few snippets, but the consensus of those that she could hear was that no one had any clue as to who the mystery woman was.

Was the victim actually a nun? Or was it possible that she was someone obsessed with the legend behind the ghost run? After all, the so-called anniversary was coming up shortly. Is it possible that this poor woman dressed up and killed herself?

Unfortunately, with everything going on in the world today, Kari really couldn't say that idea wasn't plausible, except there was one thing that bothered Kari about the whole thing; her gut. Deep in the pit of her stomach, Kari had the feeling that this was no accident.

Finally, the officer who was assigned to question Rebecca made his way over to the pair. "Excuse me, ladies. I'm Officer Sean Ward. I need to ask you two a few questions."

Officer Ward looked rather young to be working for the police department. From his boyish looks, Kari would have guessed he was barely out of high school. However, knowing that there was an age requirement meant that he had to be at least twenty-one years old.

No matter his age, the young officer was very nice. He waited for Kari to explain that she was with

Hunter when the call came in and was only here as moral support for Rebecca.

Officer Ward then directed his questions to a very silent Rebecca. It was possible she was suffering from shock; Kari couldn't be sure. She'd been alright talking to Kari, but perhaps having to give a statement to the police had pushed her further over the edge.

"Ma'am, are you up to answering a few questions?" The young officer asked.

Kari squeezed Rebecca's arm to reassure her and waited patiently until the questions were completed.

"Where were you just before the body was discovered?" Officer Ward questioned.

Thinking back over her day, Rebecca stated that she was talking to a friend via video chat in her room. "Oh no!" She exclaimed. I forgot about my friend during all the excitement. I asked her if she could hold on for a few minutes so that I could see what going on. I never hung up, I bet she still waiting for me to come back."

Officer Ward asked, "So, I take it you didn't actually see the victim fall?"

49

Shaking her head, Rebecca's eyes were darting all over, "No, thank goodness. I heard someone, Mandy Finch, I think, scream so I came running."

"How long did it take you to run down those stairs?" The young officer asked Rebecca.

"I'm not sure, five minutes maybe. Maybe less." Rebecca answered.

"And did you see anything or anyone suspicious around that time?

"No, sir." Rebecca answered then looked back over to the crime scene tape that was going up around the area containing the body. "You don't think this was an accident, do you? Rebecca questioned.

"We can't say for certain at this time. It does appear that the victim either fell or was pushed from somewhere up there," the officer pointed toward the top of the building.

Both women gasped but had nothing further to add to the officer's proclamation.

"Thank you for your time, ma'am," the officer said to Rebecca. "If you happen to remember anything else, please call the station."

"Would it be okay for me to go to my apartment now? I really need to reassure my friend that everything is okay."

"I think that will be fine. Just remember to call if you have any additional information.

Rebecca assured him that she would call if she had anything extra to add.

"Give me just a minute and I'll go with you." Kari scanned the crowd to find Hunter. Once she had his attention, Kari motioned that she was going to accompany Rebecca back to her place while Hunter worked.

Chapter 7

Kari

"Are you still there, Stella?" Rebecca called as soon as they entered her front door.

"I'm here!"

Kari heard the reply.

"What happened??"

The two hurried to the couch, where Rebecca's laptop was set up.

Her friend, a beautiful older woman with deep chestnut hair and gorgeous blue eyes, was on the screen with a worried look on her face.

"I'm so sorry, there's been an accident here on the grounds where I live," Rebecca explained to her. "I'm going to have to let you go because the police may want to talk to me some more."

"Oh, of course! No worries at all. Please let me know how it all turns out!"

Rebecca thanked her, ended the call, then took a few deep breaths.

"That was Stella Walters," she explained to Kari. "She orders a lot of custom pieces from me for her Italian restaurant in New York City. She's one of my best customers and just a total sweetheart."

"She's beautiful," Kari commented.

"Oh, yes. She modeled in Italy before she came here with her husband."

Kari was glad to see that her friend had calmed down a bit since she'd first seen her that evening. She thought it might be due to her apartment and its gorgeous décor that seemed specifically chosen to induce a tranquil mood.

It also had to help that they were now in the safety of a locked room. Kari had not missed the fact that Rebecca had immediately engaged the deadbolt as soon as they were both in the apartment.

"Are you feeling better?" Kari asked her, sitting down on the couch beside her friend.

"Yes, thank you. It was just such a shock, you know? You don't expect someone to die right outside your window! In fact, you don't expect people to die at all. Did you know this is the first time I've ever seen a dead body?"

Kari nodded in sympathy.

She remembered her first dead body. She and her sister had been the ones to find poor Lila.

It wasn't something you ever got over.

She knew she should be focused on comforting Rebecca right now, but there were a million questions buzzing through her head. And wasn't this the best time to ask them? After all, Rebecca was calm and relaxed.

If she was questioned now, she might remember things she'd never recall if she was being interviewed by the police.

You're totally justifying your behavior she chided herself, but that apparently wasn't enough to stop her.

"I saw Sam and Mandy Finch out there. How are they doing with this whole thing?"

Rebecca shook her head sadly. "They're actually the ones who discovered the body. Can you imagine? I mean, look how I reacted, and I didn't even get close to the thing! And those two are such calm, wonderful people. I'm sure it was a real shock."

"Sam and Mandy live here, right? They're the full-time residents?"

Kari thought she recalled Rebecca telling her earlier that only four units were occupied by people year-round. Others just used the Abbey as a retreat or a summer home, and some took out short-term leases for specific projects or vacations.

"Yes," Rebecca confirmed.

"Such nice people. They have a little dog named Mr. Snappy Pants that they've been training to work in commercials. They're out in the courtyard almost every single day with him. I hear them calling out instructions every morning when I get out of the shower."

Kari couldn't help but giggle at the name. "Sounds like he's made for show business!"

"Oh, definitely! You should see him dance around on his back paws. It's super cute! Sometimes, I'll open my studio windows while I work, just so I can hear his adorable little bark."

"So, Sam and Mandy live here full time, and so do you. Who are the others?"

Kari found herself scooting closer to Rebecca and realized she was being a little too eager. *Dial it down a notch. You're not an investigator, you're her friend.* She thought.

"Well, there's Penny Green and then there's Prudence Greer. Damon is Prudence's nephew from Portland and has been living with her for a couple of weeks

55

since he got hurt at work. I think Prudence really enjoys having him around. She was lonely before. Of course, a lot of artists tend to isolate themselves."

She smiled. "We think it helps us deepen our craft."

"I did notice that he was on crutches when I saw him tonight," Kari said. *No way is he taking any of the rickety staircases in any of these buildings*, she thought. "So, what does he do back in Portland?"

"Hmmm," Rebecca said, thinking.

"Pretty sure Prudence mentioned he worked in theater. I remember thinking he'd make a perfect addition to all us dramatic creative types here at the Abbey!"

"This place sure does attract those in the arts, doesn't it?" Kari asked.

Rebecca nodded enthusiastically.

"It's one of the reasons I love it so much. It can be difficult to find others who understand the creative thought process, especially in a small town like this. I love knowing I can head over to my studio and run into other people who are going through the same things as me. It's like a big creative family."

She pulled her long blond hair into a ponytail and started running her hands through it.

A big creative family that caused someone to jump off a roof,
Kari thought. *Or, does this have nothing to do with the
Abbey residents? Was it just a high school prank gone wrong,
like Hunter suggested?*

"Hey, thanks for coming up here with me, Kari."
Rebecca put her arms around her and gave her a
fierce hug. I was really thrown for a loop. If you
hadn't come up, I probably would have bawled to my
poor client on our video conference. And that's really
no way to act around a client. Poor Stella would have
been mortified."

"That's what friends are for," Kari assured her. "Are
you okay now? I'd better go find Hunter. He has to
give me a ride home, and he's probably wondering
where I wandered off to."

"Yes, I think I'll be fine now," Rebecca told her,
getting up and leading her to the door. "A glass of
chardonnay, some chocolate, and a bath, and I'll be
ready for bed!"

"Now that sounds like a winning combination," Kari
said with a laugh.

"Well, you'll have to come back for a glass under
better circumstances," Rebecca told her. "You and
your sister both."

"Okay, well, make sure you call me if you need anything. Or, if you remember anything else you think I should tell Hunter."

As she left the apartment, she heard Rebecca engage the deadbolt behind her.

I'm glad she's being safe, she thought, *but it's a shame that she feels she needs to do that now.*

Deciding to take the stairs in case the elevator in the building had the same problems as the ones in the artist's building, Kari started down the creaking steps.

She was almost halfway down when she heard some thumping coming from the stairwell under her.

Her heart sped up, and she found herself pressed against the wall. What if it was the killer?

Stop being such a wuss, she thought, shaking her head. Plenty of people lived in this building, and it was likely just another resident.

The thumping made perfect sense when she continued her descent and saw that it was Damon coming up the stairs.

"Hi, there," she greeted him brightly, but he barely looked up as they passed. *Well that was rude. And why in the world would he take the stairs when he's on crutches?*

She brushed the questions off as she walked out the door and spotted Hunter in the crowd. She was excited to tell him what she had learned from Rebecca and see if he'd figured out who their mystery nun really was.

It was certainly an action-packed night and a date to remember.

Chapter 8

Hunter

"Ugghhhh," Hunter groaned to himself. *I can't believe my luck. Things were going so well with Kari, and then, boom! This had to happen.*

It had been a little over an hour since Hunter and Kari arrived at The Abbey, but he was still no closer to identifying the deceased nor determining if this was an accident or murder. Police work could be very tedious at times.

Tonight, was one of those times.

As he turned to look for the rookie cop, Jordan, Hunter caught a glimpse of the young woman being examined by the coroner. A sudden pang of guilt crept over him as he chastised himself for putting his feelings for Kari over that of the dead girl.

She's someone's daughter, and they deserve to have her back in their arms, not lying here like this. If Kari is the right one for me, she'll understand that, sometimes, the job will interfere.

As if she knew he was thinking about her, Hunter caught a glimpse of Kari heading toward him out of the corner of his eye. His heart fluttered once again as a smile spread across her face.

In his head, Hunter could almost hear her say, "I'm sorry, this stinks for me, too."

Despite his mood, Hunter couldn't help but give her a smile in return.

"Kari, I'm so sorry about this. If I'd have known that the call was a possible homicide, I would've taken you home before coming here."

Kari frowned and said, "Don't worry about it. I'm fine. It was important for you to come as quickly as possible, and, to be honest, I really wanted to check on Rebecca. She's more than a business acquaintance, she's a friend."

"You might want to reserve your understanding nature for a little while. It looks like I'm going to be another couple of hours. If it's ok with you, I've asked Officer Jordan to escort you home whenever you're ready."

Much to Hunter's delight, Kari had a disappointed look on her face. *Maybe she really does have feelings for me*, he thought.

"I guess I'd better get home," she said, though her voice was filled with hesitation. "There's no telling what time you'll finish, and I'm afraid I'll just be in your way until then."

"Well I do find myself distracted whenever you're around," Hunter teased. He liked the way her bashfulness caused Kari's face to light up whenever he flirted with her.

"Tell the truth," Kari said, her cheeks blooming with color. "You're just trying to get out of buying me that ice cream for dessert, aren't you?"

"You caught me!"

Interrupting their flirtation, Office Jordan walked up to them, and cleared his throat.

"Excuse me, Houston, Kingston said you were looking for me?"

"Oh, yes. This is Kari Sweet. She accompanied me here tonight, and I need you to escort her home."

Hunter's eyes narrowed as he emphasized, "And, be careful, got it?"

"Yes…sir," the rookie cop stammered.

As he turned to Kari, Hunter said, "I'll make up for the ice cream another time, okay? Again, I'm sorry that work ruined our night. Call me when you get home?"

"What, don't you trust Officer Jordan here?" Kari teased.

"Stop stirring up trouble." Hunter joked.

Kari laughed as she turned to follow the confused rookie to his cruiser. Just as she was about to get inside, she called out, "Hey Hunter, just so you know, our night wasn't ruined."

Hunter stood and stared at the car's taillights as it drove away, carrying the most captivating woman he'd ever had the pleasure of taking out to dinner.

"I've got to get my head in the game!" He mumbled to himself and turned to find Officer Kingston. "Hey, Jo, tell me you got something."

"Afraid not, hon. Everyone I talked to seems to have an alibi around the time of death. It looks like we have two mysteries on our hands."

"Two? I know the obvious—who's the victim—but what's the second?" Hunter asked.

"I don't believe this young lady is a nun. So, why is she wearing a nun's habit?"

Hunter thought for a few seconds, then asked, "Why don't you think she's a nun?"

"Three things. Her hair's been dyed, her nails have been manicured, and she has make-up on, none of which nuns do. So, I think this is just some costume. Now, we need to know why."

"That's good, Jo. I noticed the make-up, but I didn't catch the hair and nails. So. I'd have to agree with you. Chances are that our victim isn't a nun. Who is she and why that get-up?"

Hunter scratched his head and looked around the perimeter once again.

"There has to be something else that we're missing. Let's go over all the statements again and see if any of them contradict each other. But let's do this back at the station. There's a lot of nosy people around here. If it was a murder, we don't want to tip our hand just yet."

"It looks like the coroner is about ready to move the body," Jo added. "We can leave a few uniforms behind and have them recanvas the area. If we need to, we can have them bring someone in for further questioning."

"Ok, I'll grab these evidence bags and meet you at your car." Hunter turned and started packing up the bags.

Once he had placed the last box in Jo's cruiser, Hunter walked over to the coroner who had finally placed the deceased in the body bag.

Like many small communities that dotted the area, Mills Township shared a medical examiner. Dr. Elwood Thurber had served the surrounding communities for as long as Hunter could remember. If he had to guess, Dr. Thurber was in his late seventies, but he acted like a much younger fortyish lady's man.

He was almost as tall as Hunter with thick salt and pepper hair that he kept slicked back in a style that was popular in the sixties.

Every time Hunter looked at the man, he thought of an old commercial his grandfather used to repeat as he was getting ready for church on Sunday mornings; "Brylcreem, just a little dab will do ya." From the amount of shine in Thurber's hair, Hunter would have to say he was using more than a dab.

"Evening, Dr. Thurber. It looks like you're about ready to move the body?"

"Hey, Hunter, it's good to see you. Sad under such circumstances, but I'm glad that you're working this one."

Hunter smiled at the old man. He was a nice guy and very good at his job. Hunter worried that at his age, it wouldn't be long before Thurber had to retire, and he'd sure miss the guy when he did.

"It's going to be a tough one. We still haven't figured out who she is. Everyone here says they don't recognize her. On top of that, Jo and I think she might not even be a nun."

Thurber nodded his head. "I'd have to agree with you. It's highly unlikely she was a nun. I've completed a initial examination, and I've found two tattoos and a belly piercing."

"Any hope that you've got a cause of death for me?"

"Now, Hunter, you know that I can't give you a definitive answer until after I've completed my autopsy." Dr. Thurber frowned at Hunter.

"I know that, Doc, I'm not wanting anything to put on paper. I just want your best guess. It might help steer me in the right direction."

"From my preliminary examination, I'd say she fell from somewhere up there." Thurber pointed toward the top of The Abbey.

"Of course, until I can do a better exam, I can't tell you if she had help or not. And, as you know, there are some medical conditions that make it easy for a person to fall on their own. Until I'm done, I won't even hazard a guess." Thurber finished and waited for Hunter to let him go.

"Thanks, Doc, it might not be enough just yet, but I'm confident that you'll find something. Just give me a call."

"You got it. By the way, who's the young lady I saw you with just now?"

"Kari Sweet..." Hunter noticed the grin on Thurber's face. "She's just a friend, so don't you start in on me, too!"

"So, what you're saying is that she's available?"

"Well now, I didn't exactly say that, did I?" Hunter quickly cut his friend off before things got a little awkward.

"Ah ha! I knew I'd get it out of you sooner or later. Don't worry. I won't move in on your lady, even if she's a looker."

Hunter chuckled at Thurber's brash behavior. The doc might pretend to be a lady's man, but everyone knew he was all talk and no action. In fact, Dr. Elwood Thurber hadn't been on a date since the death of his wife almost ten years ago.

As they parted, Hunter's thoughts were on his own future.

I hope that one day I'll have that special someone to start my life with. The kind of love Thurber had with his wife was one of a kind.

That's what he wanted in his life.

Kari just might be the one, who knows? Hunter thought.

Speaking of Kari, she hasn't called yet. I hope Officer Jordan didn't try any funny business with her. I think I'll call just to make sure.

Hopping in his truck, Hunter digs his phone out of his pocket and pulled up Kari's number.

"If that rookie tried to get fresh with you…" Hunter mumbled as he hit the send button on his phone.

He didn't complete his thought.

Chapter 9

Kari

Kari had been home for almost twenty minutes when her cell phone lit up with a call.

When she'd gotten home, she'd made herself a hot cup of cocoa and she sat in the kitchen, trying to process everything she'd seen that night.

It was tough to think that they were faced with yet another suspicious death, but she was determined to help Hunter figure out what had happened that night at the Abbey.

She grabbed her phone on the second ring and saw Hunter's name on the screen.

Oh my gosh, I completely forgot to call him! she realized. The excitement of the evening had obviously gotten to her. "I am so sorry," she said instead of 'hello'. "I got home, and I was just trying to calm down from everything that went down tonight, and I completely forgot to let you know I got home okay! Can you ever forgive me?"

Hunter laughed.

"Hey, don't worry about it! I just wanted to make sure my young officer didn't hold you hostage in the squad car while he told you how pretty you are. He looked pretty star struck when I told him he'd be taking you home. I hope that he acted professionally?"

"Whatever," Kari said with a chuckle. "He was a perfect gentleman. In fact, I think he was too embarrassed to even look at me during the entire drive!"

She laughed when she pictured the young officer's face when he'd bid her good night. His face had been so red, he'd looked like he'd spent two hours on the beach.

"How are things going there?"

Hunter sighed. "Well, it looks like my night is far from over. I need to head back to the station to work for a couple more hours."

"I bet you could use some nice black Columbian roast, huh? Good thing we didn't decide to share a bottle of wine at dinner!" Kari joked.

"No kidding! I'd be dead on my feet! Though that does sound like something we need to do soon."

Kari felt a thrill of excitement in her stomach at the thought of a future date with Hunter. There was certainly something about this man that made her feel all tingly inside.

"So, do you know yet if it was an accident or...something more sinister?" She didn't want to say the word 'murder'. It just seemed too ugly.

"Nope, not yet, and it looks like no one saw what happened. Don't worry though, it's early. I'm sure we'll get to the bottom of it soon. Of course, the first thing we need to do is find out who this girl is."

"The nun?" Kari asked.

"Oh, this is no nun."

He filled her in on the makeup, manicure, and tattoos. "Looks like she was just dressed up as one."

"Then it might have been a prank gone wrong, like you thought in the beginning?"

"I guess so, but my gut says no. I don't have anything to back it up, but I think this girl was killed on purpose."

Kari felt a sinking sensation in her stomach.

Really? Another murder in our town?

"The first step is positively identifying her," Hunter was saying. "You never know what that will bring to

71

light. There could be a whole list of people who might have wanted to do her harm."

"It's doubtful she's from here, right?" Kari asked him. "I mean, someone would have recognized her or reported her missing if she was a local."

"We can't rule that out for sure yet. I didn't recognize her, but I don't know every person in town. And this just happened tonight, so it's possible her family or friends don't even know she's missing."

"Oh, that girl's poor family!" Kari had a vision of what it would be like if it were Kasi lying on that cold ground. The thought almost made her sick. *Speaking of Kasi, where is she? I haven't heard a peep from her since I got home.*

She and Hunter continued to chat until he got to the station.

"I'll stop by the shop tomorrow and give you an update on what we found," he told her before they hung up. "You try to get a good night's sleep, okay?"

She said she would and ended the call.

Even though their date had been interrupted by a dead body, she still felt pretty good about it.

They always had so much to talk about, and she had to admit she felt safe and cared for when she was with him.

"Someone's out late!" Kasi walked into the kitchen and gave her a mischievous grin.

"I stayed up in my room just in case you wanted to do some canoodling in the kitchen."

Kari shook her head.

"No canoodling for this girl. Our date got interrupted by a corpse."

She quickly filled her sister in on the dead woman dressed like a nun that had cut their date short.

"I can't believe this!" Kasi exclaimed when she finished. "Everyone has been talking about the whole ghost nun anniversary, but I don't think anyone expected something like this to happen!"

"I know," Kari agreed.

"I keep thinking it was just an accident or something, but Hunter seems to think there was foul play."

"Well, I would trust him if I were you. He's seen a lot more of this than we have."

"Not a lot more," Kari reminded her. "Until not long ago, the most exciting case he'd had was some drunk high school kid holding up the local gas station."

"True," Kasi said with a nod, "but I still think he has good instincts. What does Rebecca think?"

"She was pretty shaken up," Kari told her.

"She doesn't seem to think it could be anyone that lives there. They all seem tight because most of them are artists or trying to break into show business. She said they're like a big family."

"Maybe it's not someone who lives there," Kasi mused.

"It would take a pretty brash criminal to kill someone right on their own property. I'm thinking she was probably lured there."

The two chatted about possible scenarios for a few more minutes before Kasi steered the conversation back to her date.

"So, did you at least enjoy yourself before you had to go investigate a dead body?"

Kari nodded. "He's really great, Kasi. You know how I always found it hard to talk to my boyfriends in college?"

Kasi rolled her eyes. "Oh, yeah. I remember one guy, in particular. I think you brought him home for Christmas your junior year."

"Jacob," Kari said, cringing at the name. "Yeah, he was a real winner."

"You definitely had a type," Kasi confirmed.

"And that type tended to be smug, self-satisfied men who thought they were smarter than everyone else."

"I think I mistook that for actually being intelligent," Kari told her. "It took me a long time to figure out that the guys who tried to act the smartest were just the opposite."

"Well, Hunter isn't like that at all," Kasi told her. "You can tell he's comfortable in his own skin."

Kari bobbed her head enthusiastically. "He's definitely that. And so easy to talk to. He seems interested in almost every subject you can imagine, and I love his sense of humor."

Kasi smiled and put her arm around her.

"I'm proud of you, big sis. I think you might finally be growing up." She stifled a yawn and added, "You know, as much as I'm enjoying this, I think I might have to hit the sack. You know it's going to be busy at the shop tomorrow."

"Oh, yeah. You know how this town gets after there's a dead body. People are going to come from miles around to be part of the action."

"And, they're going to need coffee," Kasi confirmed. "And maybe some delicious baked goods. I hate to say we're going to profit from someone dying, but we have to be prepared."

Kari gave her sister a hug good night before changing and settling herself into her comfy bed.

She expected to have trouble falling asleep after everything that transpired that night, but she quickly fell into a deep slumber.

The problem was that her sleep was interrupted by disturbing dreams in which she was being chased by monks and walnut bread-wielding nuns.

Right before she woke up, the monk pushed her off the roof of the Abbey.

Chapter 10

Kari

"Today is going to be rough. I don't think I got an hour's worth of good sleep last night," Kari said, stifling a yawn as she backed out of their driveway. "Not only did I toss and turn all night, but I kept having weird dreams."

"Let me guess, you dreamed of nuns, didn't you?" Kasi asked.

"Something like that."

The sisters were headed to the coffee shop early the next morning. They hoped to get several loaves of warm walnut bread ready before customers start to arrive.

"If it makes you feel any better, I didn't sleep all that well, either. The thought of us tangled up in another murder investigation kind of scares me."

Kasi looked at her sister with a worried expression.

"To be honest, it makes me a little nervous, too. But the thing is, when your life was in danger, I would have done anything to protect you, even if that meant putting myself in danger as well. I can't help but think that someone needs to stand up for that poor girl."

"Oh, I agree, Kari. I'm just saying that until this mystery is solved, I won't get a good night's sleep."

The girls were quiet for a few moments, then Kari broke the silence to broach a subject that she feared might make Kasi a little uncomfortable.

"Hey, I know we really don't talk too much about you being stalked, but I want you to know if you ever need anything, I'm here for you."

Kasi looked at her sister and smiled. "I know, but don't worry. I'm fine. Occasionally, I find myself looking over my shoulder, but I refuse to be afraid."

"That's good, but if you need to talk, I'm here."

"I know and thanks!" Kasi said.

The last few minutes of the ride to the coffee shop were uneventful, and soon, the sisters were busy in the small kitchen.

The scent of walnut bread gently wafted throughout the building, giving it that warm, homey feeling that so many of their customers enjoyed.

Kari looked over her shoulder at the clock hung on the wall and saw that it was five minutes until the scheduled opening time.

"Wow, I guess that old saying is true, time flies when you're having fun. Time to open the door."

"Oh, you're right. It feels like we just got here. I have one more pan in the oven. Can you get the door, and I'll be out in a minute?"

"Take your time. I don't expect the rush for a little while longer."

Much to Kari's surprise, when she got to the front door, a line had already formed and was waiting for the door to be unlocked.

She quickly flipped the open sign on and unlatched the door.

The first person who came in was Flossie Thompkins.

Flossie was an older widow who lived just a block from the shop. She loved Kasi's chicken salad so much that she came in at least once a week to indulge.

Since her second favorite thing to do at the shop was to gossip, it was no surprise that the first thing she said to Kari was, "Did you hear about the nun that was murdered at the Abbey yesterday?"

"Good morning, Miss. Flossie. Unfortunately, I already know about the suspicious death."

Flossie plopped down at her usual table and began to tell Kari how awful it was that some poor girl died just because of some ghost story.

"Now, Miss. Flossie," Kari began, "no one knows exactly what happened last night, so I wouldn't believe any rumors just yet."

"But it isn't a rumor, Kari dear. My nephew who lives out that way told my sister that there are young kids all the time sneaking into that property, trying to catch a glimpse of the ghost nun."

"Did your nephew say if he saw trespassers there last night?"

Kasi had walked into the dining room just in time to hear Flossie's news.

"Well, no," she stammered. "Roy has been in Chicago since last week on a business trip, but that doesn't mean there weren't kids there last night. After all, the anniversary of the ghost nun is coming up."

The sisters smiled sweetly at Flossie. They knew she meant well, but good intentions weren't going to help Hunter solve this case even if it was true about kids trespassing at The Abbey.

"So, Miss. Flossie, what can I get you this morning? We have some fresh baked walnut bread," Kari said, hoping to change the subject.

"Oh, that sounds heavenly! And I'll have one of those vanilla latte things you introduced me to last week. I hope it'll make my tummy think I'm eating ice cream.

I'm on a diet, so I've got to watch me eating too much sugar."

Kasi snickered, soliciting a stern look from her sister.

"Sure thing, Miss. Flossie!"

Kari didn't have the heart to tell such a sweet lady that a bowl of ice cream probably had less sugar than what she was about to consume.

If it had been anyone else, she would have burst that bubble, but Flossie was in perfect health and couldn't weigh more than a hundred and ten pounds soaking wet. Plus, she knew Flossie well enough to know that Flossie didn't really want to know.

For the next hour, the girls listened to customers discuss every aspect of the mysterious case.

Several people, like Flossie, didn't bother to wait for the police to put out an official statement and felt it was their duty to make wild speculations.

Later that morning, Kasi overheard an unknown woman who lived in a town less than an hour away talking about the incident.

She was passing through on the way to Detroit but had decided to stop in for a quick bite before settling in for a long trip. The woman had turned around in her seat to talk to two other women who had been discussing the "nun's" death.

"You know how young kids these days are," she said wisely. "Always wanting to go viral on social media. Makes no sense to me. In my day, a virus was something you avoided, now everyone wants to go out and get viral."

"You're so right," one of the other women agreed. "My daughter thinks that the couple dressed as a nun and a monk to make a video reenacting the Ghost Nun, and they got into an argument, and he just went nuts and pushed her off the roof."

Kasi had been wiping off a table next to the two groups and had been listening intently to the conversations.

Seeing her opportunity, she politely said, "Excuse me, ma'am. I've been here all day and haven't heard anything new. Did you say they know the identity of the young woman who died?"

"Not that I know of, why?"

"Because you said that your daughter thought the couple had an argument."

"Well, of course. Why else would someone push a girl off the roof unless they were arguing?"

Kasi was getting frustrated but trying not to show it. "I'm sorry. I'm a little confused. Who reported that there was a man dressed as a monk?"

The woman stood up and grabbed her check.

"I have no idea. My daughter saw some people talking about it on Facebook, and she told me about it before I left home."

"So, what you're repeating is a rumor your daughter heard?" Kasi asked, surprised.

"I'll have you to know I don't spread rumors! I was just telling this nice lady what my daughter heard from a friend. I think you should be more concerned about doing your job and less about eavesdropping on your customers!"

The woman stomped over to the register and slapped her bill down on the counter in front of Kari. "You know, you guys should be ashamed of yourselves, making a profit from a poor girl's death."

Completely confused, Kari replied, "I'm sorry, I have no idea what you're talking about."

"That sign you have out front with the monk on it. You're using that murdering monk's image to boost your business, and I think it's tacky."

Her voice carried heavily across the room, and people stopped talking and started to stare.

Knowing that this kind of situation could ruin the coffee shops reputation, Kari decided to act. "I'm so sorry you feel that way, but let me assure you, the sign out front was commissioned from a local artist way before incident last night. It's purely coincidental. Kasi, why don't you wrap up a warm slice of walnut bread and a cappuccino to go, on the house, of course. We don't want our customers thinking we'd ever do something so underhanded just for a profit."

"Why thank you," the woman said, pulling back her shoulders and tossing back her hair. "It's refreshing to see young people who know the cardinal rule in the service industry, the customer is always right."

As soon as Kasi handed the cranky customer the packaged bread and coffee, she turned and left the shop.

"What in the world just happened?" Kasi asked her sister.

"A misunderstanding, it's not important right now," Kari told her. "It looks like you're running low on walnut bread. Do you mind bringing some more out while I shuffle a few things around in our display case?"

Kari heard the bell ring over the door as someone entered but didn't turn around to see who it was. She really needed a break from all the gossiping that was going on.

Suddenly, Kari heard Kasi psst her from the doorway.

"Kari, your boyfriend is here," She said in that sing-song voice she reserved for announcing Hunter.

As she tried to hide the huge smile that crept across her face, Kari thought, Just what I needed to brighten my day!

She looked over Kasi's shoulder and caught a glimpse of Hunter standing at the counter.

He looked worn out.

"I bet he's been up most of the night working on this case."

Once again, a smile replaced the frown she'd worn after seeing Hunter's expression.

"I think I know someone who needs a pick me up, and I know just what to give him."

Chapter 11

Kari

"Well, hello there, handsome," Kari said as she sauntered up the count to greet Hunter. "I think I know exactly what to do to make your day."

Whoa, that came out a little racier than I'd intended, she thought.

Hunter looked perplexed for a moment, then broke out into a big grin. "Oh, really?" he said. "Do tell."

She shook her head and chuckled.

"I meant that I was going to get coffee for you and your whole crew at the station. I know how hard you've all been working on this case."

Hunter held his hands up to his chest and heaved a big, dramatic sigh.

"You're breaking my heart, Ms. Sweet."

"Give me a break, you two," Kasi muttered from behind them. "You're acting like lovesick teenagers, and it's making me a little queasy."

"You're just jealous!" Hunter hollered at her as she went into the back room. He turned his eyes back to

Kari. "We should find someone to set your sister up with. I think she's lonely."

"Yeah, that never works out well," Kari told him, recalling the one and only time she'd tried to arrange a date for Kasi.

Her sister had stood him up in favor of watching a good movie on TV while eating ice cream in her footie pajamas.

If there was one thing Kasi Sweet was not, it was lonely for a man. She'd found one she actually liked, and he was killed. There was no way Kasi was in a hurry to fall for another guy.

"So what time did you get home from the station last night?" she asked, eager to turn the conversation back to the case.

"I never left," he told her, running a hand through his hair. "I grabbed a quick shower at the station and a nap on one of the couches."

He rolled his shoulders a couple of times. "That thing is not comfortable. I think I might have slipped a disk or something."

"They have a shower at the station?" Kari asked. "I didn't know that."

"Where do you think the prisoners shower?" Hunter asked.

"Oh, jeez. You had to shower in there? Isn't that a little…unsettling?"

Hunter laughed. "It's not like they were in there with me! But yeah, it wasn't exactly a relaxing spa experience."

Kari cringed. "I'm really sorry. You guys need caffeine even more than I thought! And sugar. Looks like I'll have to throw some walnut bread in with your coffee."

As she busied herself with brewing a new pot of coffee, she filled Hunter in on the gossip she'd heard in the shop earlier that morning.

"You think there's any truth to those rumors?" she asked him when she'd finished summing up the conversation.

Hunter shrugged. "Sounds like a lot of conjecture mixed with rumors to me," he said. "Everyone loves a good ghost story, and you can bet that plenty of people want to embellish what happened just for a scare. This whole social media thing is just complicating matters. I wouldn't put any stock in it."

"You still don't know who the girl is?" Kari asked, pouring the freshly made brew into a huge to-go container.

She wondered if she should brew a second pot for them. It certainly sounded like they needed it.

Hunter shook his head. "Nope, we haven't gotten a solid ID yet, and it's making me crazy. She's got a family out there somewhere wondering where she is, and I feel terrible that we can't help them."

Kari nodded, putting some freshly baked walnut bread and biscotti from their friend Jenna's bakery in Maine into a box.

After closing it up, she slipped some more bread into a smaller box and handed it to Hunter. "Why don't you hide this one somewhere just for you? I have a feeling the rest of the boys down at the station will go through the big box pretty quickly."

Hunter gave her a wink. "You know just how to take care of me, don't you?"

Kari felt herself flush. What was it with their intense flirting today? Were they really taking their relationship to that next level?

And was she ready for that?

"Well, you can't do good investigative work on an empty stomach," she told him. "Any other clues since last time we talked?"

He shook his head. "Nothing. Every time we think we have something; it just leads to another dead end."

"What about the autopsy?" Kari asked.

"We won't get the results until later today," Hunter explained. "I'm not sure how helpful it'll be, though. Clearly, she died from the fall."

"You never know," Kari mused. "She could have been poisoned or drugged or something. Or maybe smacked on the head and knocked out before she was pushed?"

"All good points," Hunter said, nodding his head. "Hmm, there's a reason I keep bringing you in on cases. I like how your mind works."

Kari's blush deepened. "Well, I just call it like I see it."

She pulled a big paper bag out from under the counter and started loading it with coffee cups, sugar, creamer, and the pastry boxes.

"Anything else you need?" she asked when the bag was full to the brim.

"I can't imagine," Hunter said with a chuckle, pulling out his wallet.

"How much is this going to set me back?"

She waved him away. "On the house, Officer Hunter. I have to do what I can to help out on this investigation, and right now, what I can do is provide breakfast for a bunch of hungry cops."

"Aww, that's really nice of you, Kari. I know everyone at the station will appreciate it." He grabbed the bag in one hand and the large container of coffee in the other. "I'll call or text you later to fill you in on the autopsy and anything else we find out."

Kari waved good-bye to him as he hauled his goodies out of the shop and to his truck.

She heard a giggle behind her when Hunter almost dropped the coffee as he tried to open the driver's side door.

"You're in trouble, sis," she said when Kari turned around to look at her.

"What do you mean?" Kari asked innocently.

"An adorable cop who is totally smitten with you? Sheesh. I can hear the wedding bells a 'ringing already!"

Kari shook her head and snapped the kitchen towel at her younger sister. "We haven't even really been on a proper date," she reminded her. "I wouldn't be planning the bachelorette party just yet."

"You forget, I've known you almost your whole life," Kasi pointed out, starting to mix up another batch of walnut bread to put in the oven.

"I've never seen you act this way around anyone you've ever dated. I'm telling you, sis, I think this is the one."

Kari started grabbing more of the ingredients Kasi would need for the bread and set them beside the mixing bowl.

"I have to be honest, right now, I'm more concerned with who the dead fake nun is than I am in my future marital status. Can you imagine your daughter disappearing and having no idea she was dead?"

Or your sister?

The thought came into her head unbidden, and she tried to push it away. She couldn't even contemplate the idea of something happening to Kasi. It was just too horrible to think about.

Kasi stirred thoughtfully for a few seconds, then shook her head. "Maybe she's a runaway or something. She might not have any family at all. That could be one of the reasons we're having such a tough time identifying her."

Kari wondered if that made the situation better or worse. The thought of a grieving mother was awful, but the thought of a young girl having absolutely no one who cared about her was just as bad.

"I'm sure we'll find out sooner or later," she told her. "I just hope it's sooner."

She looked up when the bell over the door rang and a stream of customers came in.

The lunch rush had officially begun, and they wouldn't have time to think about the unidentified girl for at least a couple of hours.

Kari, for one, welcomed the distraction.

"Welcome to On Bitter Grounds!" Kasi trilled to the new customers. "I hope I can interest you all in some delicious walnut bread. I just took a new pan out of the oven!"

The girls busied themselves filling orders, but Kari found herself looking repeatedly at her phone.

The call from Hunter with the autopsy results could come at any moment, and she was determined not to miss it.

Chapter 12

Hunter

"I smell food," a young officer all but shouted. "And fresh coffee. Who went out for lunch and didn't tell me?"

Everyone looked puzzled as they surveyed the others in the room, hoping to find the culprit.

Jo Kingston laughed and pointed to the door Hunter was having trouble opening, "If someone doesn't help him with the door, all those things y'all are drooling over are going to end up on the floor."

Instantly, four bodies rushed forward, one grabbing the door while the other three relieved Hunter of the packages he was struggling to keep upright.

Seeing the individual box Kari fixed him in the hands of one of the officers, Hunter grabbed it and said, "Hands off. That one's all mine!"

"Possession is nine-tenths of the law," the junior officer teased.

Hunter shot him a look that threatened bodily harm, inspiring him to quickly hand over the box.

"But since you did go to all the trouble of thinking of us, I guess you should get first dibs," he said sheepishly.

Still eyeballing the daring officer, Hunter casually took the box and said, "See to it that this doesn't happen again." Then he strolled to his desk and tucked the box inside his file cabinet for safe keeping.

Turning to face the sound of good-natured fighting over the still warm bread, Hunter couldn't help but smile at those around him. They worked together, ate together and spent countless hours with one another, and he couldn't imagine his life without his partners.

It was true about law enforcement becoming a family after being together for a while.

"Hey Houston," Officer Jordan shouted, "If this is how your girlfriend treats all your friends, I vote you keep her around for a while!"

Hunter quickly threw a wadded-up napkin at the young officer's head and said, "Mind your own business, Jordan!"

Jo motioned for Hunter to join her on the far side of the room. "I thought I'd let the guys have a break for a little bit. They've been following one crappy lead after another all day."

"I know what you mean. I took a call from someone earlier who said that the dead girl was her aunt." Hunter said.

"Oh, really," Jo said with a rueful laugh.

"Yep, it seems the aunt went missing a few years ago and since the description of the victim was similar to the aunt, she thought it could be her." Hunter said.

"Wow, I didn't realize that we had any open missing persons cases?"

"We don't. The aunt is a drugged-out stripper in south Florida. We've come to find out the girl's mother only told her daughter that her aunt disappeared rather than tell her the truth." Hunter frowned. "The cat's out of the bag now."

"Well now, that's one for the books. But don't let that get you down." Jo waved a sheet of paper under Hunter's nose. "We finally caught a break in the case!"

"Tell me we've got an identification for our Jane Doe?"

"You bet! We expanded our search nationwide and IAFIS finally came through for us." Jo grinned as she handed Hunter a photocopy of an Oregon driver's license.

"Who do we have here?" Hunter paused to inspect the paper. "Kelsey Moore of Portland, Oregon?"

"That's her," Jo confirmed.

With a quizzical expression on his face, Hunter stated, "Now isn't that a coincidence. Didn't we interview someone who was visiting from Portland?"

"I do believe you are correct, officer." Jo had a big smile on her face.

Flipping through his note pad, Hunter smiled when he got to the section he was looking for. "The nephew of one of the residents at the Abbey, Damon Greer. Didn't he work in a theater in Portland?"

"Yep. But it gets better. The reason our Miss Moore here had her prints in the national database was because she was a member of a theatrical troupe who recently performed for the Vice President." Jo's grin widened as she sat down in the chair closest to her.

"Well now, talk about a coincidence. Somehow, I don't think that the theatre community in Portland is so large that these two haven't at least run into each other. During his interview, Damon didn't mention that he might know her, or even say that she at least looked familiar. What about the second interview later that night? Did he say anything then?" Hunter asked.

"Nope, not a thing. Funny how that happens, isn't it?"

"Very funny. I think we need to have another conversation with Mr. Greer of Portland, Oregon ASAP." Hunter smiled at Jo as he picked up a dry erase marker and headed to the board in the conference room."

"Jordan, grab someone and come here. Houston and I have a job for you." Jo called across the room.

***

Hunter closed the door to the conference room and looked at the murder board. Before now, all that it contained was basic information. Finally, he would be able to add something tangible.

He erased the notation of Jane Doe and replaced it with Kelsey Moore. Then he filled in the areas for date of birth and address. The cause of death had already been filled in, but the area reserved for suspects was blank.

Hunter wrote Damon Greer and then noted the connections between him and the deceased. Once he was finished, Hunter stood back and looked at the board for moment.

"I wonder if Damon Greer has a criminal record?" Hunter said to the picture on the white board.

Quickly, he walked over to his desk and accessed the NCIC database. "Okay, Mr. Greer, let's see if you're in here."

After a few minutes of searching, Hunter was able to find several Damon Greers in Oregon, but only one around the Portland area.

Following a look over the record, which was slim at best, Hunter sat back discouraged. Seeing Jo heading his way, he jotted a few notes down and ended his session on the database.

"Hey, Jordan just radioed in that he is five minutes out with Damon Greer. Anything you need me to do before he gets here?" Jo asked.

"Not too much to do, that I can see. I checked NCIC for any records in Oregon, but so far, nothing came up except a few moving violations. Of course, that really doesn't mean anything."

Together, they walked back into the conference room where Hunter added a few details from the database.

"Well, let me call Portland PD. It's possible our Mr. Greer has been on someone's radar but not actually charged with anything. He wouldn't be in the system then. If anything comes in while we're interviewing him, I will tell one of the guys to come get us."

Hunter sighed.

"It doesn't hurt to check. I don't mind pushing this guy, but I'd like to have something with some bite to push with."

"Very funny, Houston. I've seen you make want-to-be thugs cry for their mommies with just that stare of yours."

Hunter chuckled at the thought of the last boy he had in "the box".

A few months back, there had been a rash of graffiti popping up around town on buildings and bridges. Shortly afterward, a few cars were vandalized, and stores reported an uptick in shoplifting.

Rumor was that some small-time gangster had moved into the area trying to set up his own crew and was instigating some unruly behavior in the boys at the local high school.

Hunter hauled a few in along with their mentor. It didn't take long before all the boys admitted to the crimes and not only vowed to clean up their mess, but they promised to leave the gangster life behind.

All, except for their leader.

Ronald Jackson, otherwise known as Rusty Jackson or RJ, was sent from Philly by his older cousin who was the head of a small gang looking to expand their territory.

From the moment he was brought in, RJ was all attitude, or so he thought. Somehow, he had the impression he was going to walk away squeaky clean with his loyal boys taking the fall for everything.

That is, until Hunter cornered them.

By the time Hunter was done with them, those impressionable young boys were more than willing to flip on RJ. At least two of the boys broke down into tears after spending twenty minutes with Hunter just staring at them.

After it was all said and done, everyone confessed to the crimes that were known about and even a few that wasn't.

Unfortunately for RJ, who was now awaiting trial on drugs and racketeering charges, Hunter was able to put the fear of God in those boys and Mills Township is a little safer.

Well, that was until the murder of Kelsey Moore.

It will be a safe place again once I solve this case, Hunter thought.

Just then, Jordan walked into the squad room with Damon Greer in tow and led him to one of the interview rooms.

"Ready to break him?" Jo asked.

Hunter nodded, a devilish grin sliding across his face. "Like a wild horse!"

Chapter 13

Kari

"I heard it was some sort of voodoo ritual."

"My sister in Boston said something exactly like this happened there, and it had to do with a cult initiation."

"I bet it's connected to that new church that just opened two towns over. Those people don't seem right to me."

Kari and Kasi overheard dozens of theories of what could be behind the fake nun's death as they worked steadily throughout the day. At each new wild conjecture, they'd catch each other's eyes and try to hide smirks.

"If you listen to these people, we're right in the middle of some bizarre Bermuda Triangle of witchcraft and homicidal maniacs," Kasi said when the two of them met in the back room to replenish supplies.

"I know," Kari said, smoothing down her hair. With how busy they'd been, she barely had time to look in the mirror and see that her unruly curly locks were a disaster. "Why do you think people like to gossip so much?"

Kasi shrugged and pulled a bag of Vienna roast beans off the shelf. "Fear of the unknown would be my guess. It keeps their minds occupied so they don't have to think about the very real death of a young girl that happened in their backyard."

Kari shook her head with admiration. She sometimes marveled at her sister and wondered if she would've been better off going into psychology rather than business. Of course, that would mean she wouldn't get to work with her every day, so she was glad Kasi had chosen the business route.

"And it's such a weird case," Kasi continued. "A girl we can't identify dressed up as a nun falling to her death from an old convent? I mean, come on. This is the stuff gossip dreams are made of!"

"I just wish there was something we could do to help," Kari told her as they both grabbed bags of beans and headed back out to the front room. After she said it, a plan started to form in her head.

The plan continued to percolate as the girls handled the end of the lunch rush and the string of customers that kept streaming in throughout the afternoon.

The girls chatted easily with the locals and tried to keep the conversation limited to topics unrelated to the death. Many of their regulars seemed to be relieved to talk about the weather or how their kids were doing rather than to speculate on the investigation.

"I just want our low-key friendly town back," Jessica Frantz, who worked at the bank two streets over, commented as she got her coffee. "We've started locking the doors even when we're in the house, and my husband has talked about getting a security system."

Kari shook her head in sympathy. "I know, we're all a little scared. But I'm sure Hunter and his boys will have this solved in no time and we can go back to how things were."

"I hope so," Jessica said, dropping a dollar into the tip jar. "But sometimes you can't ever go back, you know? Maybe this is just our new normal."

Kari had little time to think about that as Jessica was replaced at the counter by a group of people with a big video camera and press passes. They had been talking in low voices about the case but stopped to order shots of espresso and pastries. *I wonder what they know?* Kari pondered as she took their orders.

"Can you believe how busy we've been?" Kasi asked when there was a short lull in the action. "I did a quick check of our receipts and we're up almost $2000 from a normal weekday. That's just crazy!"

"I hate to say it, but the death has been great for our business. I just wish we could figure out a way to drive tourism like this without anyone having to die." Kari looked around and saw that they were down to one customer, a local elderly man named Henry Hobbes who liked to sip a blonde roast and do a crossword puzzle in the shop every afternoon. "Hey, come here," she whispered to her sister.

Kasi raised an eyebrow and sidled up to her. "What's up?"

"I have a plan," Kari whispered, though she knew the whole cloak and dagger act was highly unnecessary. As well as being 80 years old, Henry was also nearly deaf and had no chance of overhearing their conversation.

"What kind of plan?" Kasi whispered back, excitement in her eyes.

"I was thinking we could head over to the Abbey after we close up, and maybe see if we can find out where the nun fell from."

"Ooooh, Hunter would hate that!" Kasi said with a sly grin. "I'm totally in!"

"Well, no reason to tell Hunter. If anyone sees us, we'll just say we're visiting Rebecca to make sure she's doing okay."

"And I bet she can get us up on the roof," Kasi said, nodding in approval. "Good thinking, sis. I'm getting tired of waiting around for something to happen in this case. Even if we don't find anything, at least we'll feel like we're doing something to help."

"Exactly," Kari said, glad she and her sister were on the same page. She knew that sometimes a casual visit to the scene of the crime could turn up more than with the official investigation since the residents didn't feel the pressure of law enforcement. Besides, even if they didn't find out anything that would help, they could at least see if Rebecca had remembered anything else from the night in question.

The rest of the afternoon dragged on as the girls anticipated closing time and the launch of their plan. They poured coffee and served walnut bread to a host of strangers who were obviously there for the case and watched as their receipt pile continued to grow.

Five minutes before closing time, Kasi jogged out to bring their sign in and Kari heard her give a cry of dismay.

"What's wrong?" Kari called out, her heart skipping a beat. "Are you okay?"

"Yes, but our sign isn't." Kasi walked in, dragging the chalkboard behind her. "Look at what some jerk did to our monk!"

107

Kari sighed when she saw that someone had scrawled, *Profiting from a dead girl is WRONG* over the artwork that Rebecca had so carefully created. "Who would do something like that?" she asked.

"And right in broad daylight, too," Kasi added, pulling the defiled sign behind the counter. "We'll have to ask around and see if anyone saw anything."

"And then, do what?" Kari asked. "It's on the sidewalk so it's technically public property. I don't think we can prosecute someone for writing on our chalkboard."

"Yeah, but I could go find them and crack some skulls," Kasi said in her best tough guy voice, causing her sister to burst out laughing. "What? I could punch someone if I really wanted to!"

"Oh, sure, mm hmm." Kari knew her sister had never so much as slapped someone in her entire life. The smile dropped off her face, though, when she looked closer at the sign. "There's no way to erase that without ruining Rebecca's work. We're going to have to get the sign re-done."

"Might be for the best anyway," Kasi pointed out. "Besides, it's almost time for a new special anyway. Why don't we take this with us when we head out to her place? Another good excuse for visiting the Abbey."

"Excellent idea!"

The girls finished cleaning up the shop and served the last customers of the day before turning the sign to 'Closed' and locking up for the night.

Between the two of them, they hauled the sign into the back of Kari's jeep before hopping in to head off on their adventure.

"Can you believe we're actually trying to solve a crime?" Kasi asked as Kari turned into the road that would lead them to the Abbey.

Excitement is one thing, Kari thought as she drove, *but danger is another. Let's just hope I'm not putting my sister at risk with this crazy plan.*

Chapter 14

Kari

"Hey, we need a soundtrack for our super-heroine adventure." Kari nodded at the radio but kept both hands on the wheel as she turned a corner, leaving the downtown area for more residential streets.

"On it!" Kasi turned up the volume knob. "What do ya' think, a little classic seventies rock, Charlie's Angels style?" She made her fingers into a gun shape.

Kari giggled, "Nah, there's only two of us. And besides, we don't need a Charlie to tell us what to do!"

"Alright then, Buffy and Willow! A little more modern and still a classic, unbeatable duo."

"Now you're talking!"

Kasi clicked through the preset buttons, skimming across a few commercials before hitting a station that was playing one of the late Harry Jones's dance tunes.

"Yes!" Kasi raised her hands and started dancing from the waist up in her seat. Kari just bobbed her head as she kept her eyes on the road and started singing along.

The peppy music took Kari's mind off all the troubles of Mills Township. It even seemed to lift the little aches in her body from working hard and being on her feet all day as she moved her shoulders to the tune and tapped her left foot to the beat.

She looked around at the passing landscape in the afternoon light, the fall leaves lit up in gold and copper by the autumn sun as it was beginning to near the horizon. The houses too looked precious with their weathered wood siding or brickwork with white trim. The huge Red Oak and graceful Maple trees lining the street swayed in the wind as if they were dancing to the music too.

But then the dance beat dropped off and a new song came on, this one a much slower melody on piano.

"Aww, buzz kill." Kasi started to reach for the radio buttons again, but Kari shooed her away with one hand.

"No, no, I like that song! It's Coldplay." She started to sing as her sister tilted her head and smiled at her.

Kasi rolled her eyes. "This is so you and Hunter right now."

Kari gaped at her in mock affront. "Stay out of my head, that's why I like it. And you say that like it's a bad thing. I thought you liked a good love song as much as me?"

"Really? All these lyrics about running in circles and what not? That's you guys to a tee. You just can't get together already!"

"Nobody said it was easy!" Kari sang along in answer.

"Yeah, but nobody said it had to be this hard. You've got it bad for that boy, but you won't take it to the next level."

Kasi tried to dodge as Kari punched her in the shoulder, but she couldn't move far enough in the car seat.

"Hey, I think Hunter and I are in a really good place. We've hung out a few times and had a lot of fun. I can't think of anything negative that's happened between us. Well, except for the murder cases that keep interrupting." This time Kari rolled her eyes.

"See what I mean?" Kasi leaned forward, holding out her hands. "At this rate you're never gonna get anywhere if all you ever talk about is murder suspects and dead bodies."

Kari sighed and started singing along again, the lyrics suddenly perfect, if in an ironic way.

Kasi sat back in her seat and nodded sagely, her point proven. Both sisters burst out laughing at themselves.

Kari sighed, "I know things are going a little slow now. But I can deal with it. Hunter loves his job, and he's good at it. And I love that he takes care of the community so much. If that means I have to sit and wait for him sometimes, I think it's worth it. At least, that's how I feel now. Who knows, maybe I'll change my mind in the future if his work keeps him away from me too much?" Kari said.

"I think everybody in Mills Township would agree, we'd all be happier if the police didn't have so much to keep them busy around here."

"Right on, little sister. Okay, we're here!"

As they parked beside the Abbey and hopped out of the Jeep, the upbeat vibe of the music and the beauty of the afternoon came into stark contrast with the vivid yellow lines of police crime scene tape, it's bold black letters demanding "Do Not Cross." Kari felt her stomach clench as the seriousness of the situation at hand came back into focus.

This was no scavenger hunt or game of Clue. This was a real crime scene, the site of a young woman's death. The sisters looked at each other, then together took a deep breath and pressed forward.

"Let's look around out here first." Kari suggested.

"Good call." Kasi started walking in the opposite direction from the front gate. "We know nobody inside recognized the girl in the nun costume, so she probably wasn't a guest who was invited in."

"Exactly, she must have come in another way." Kari followed, looking around at the landscaping, though much was covered in fallen leaves. "I don't remember seeing another gate in the back. Maybe we can find tracks, or maybe she had some kind of ladder she used to climb in?"

"Could be, though I think she would have lifted it inside with her, so she could use it again to get to the roof, you know? That would mean it's on the other side of the wall, like behind the building."

Kari rubbed her chin thoughtfully. "She could have, but all that would be hard to do in a nun outfit. Unless she put it on after she got inside. Maybe she left a bag for her costume stashed somewhere?"

"So many possibilities to think about." Kasi said.

"I know. Let's see what we can find." She kept in stride with Kasi.

They both left the sidewalk near the road in favor of sticking close to the base of the wall. As they went, they bent to sweep the dry leaves aside and checked behind the bushes and hedges where anything could be hidden. There were a couple of small gates around the back side, but they were well-tended wrought iron, not a spot of rust on them, and locked up tight from the inside.

As they came around the far side of the property, Kasi gasped, "Wow, look at that tree!"

"How can I not look at it? It's huge." Kari said.

To one side of the Abbey wall was a Monterey Cypress with a broad trunk and thick branches that sprawled in all directions. Its needles were a pleasant green among all the golden and orange fall hardwoods, but many of the branches were hung with curling, gray moss, making it look a little creepy. The roots curled and gnarled over each other, and the bricks at the base of the wall were beginning to give way to the massive plant's patient relentlessness. The sidewalk on the other side of the tree was even worse, despite being much newer and several feet away.

"I could see it from the parking area, but I would have sworn from there it was at least two trees together." Kari looked it up and down. "It must have been planted a hundred years ago."

"Oh my gosh, maybe they planted it when the nun died! I think I read somewhere that Cypress trees represent death."

"You and your trivia, Kasi. Here, give me a leg up."

"What?" Kasi asked.

115

Kari walked in a circle around the tree trunk, taking care not to trip over the roots. She scrutinized each of the lower branches for which would be easier to grab and strong enough to hold her weight.

"I can climb up and look over the wall. Maybe I can get a good look at the roof from up there. Besides, this might be how the girl snuck onto the property-- or how her killer did." Kari looked back at her sister with a sinister smile.

"Oh, yeah, let's climb up in the death tree. That's a great idea." Kasi put her hands on her hips. "You can't be serious, sis!"

"Come on, sissy, the tree isn't going to kill me. If anything, gravity will!" Kari said.

"That's not funny."

"You know I'll be careful. Come here and help me!"

With a frustrated hrrrgh, Kasi joined Kari by the side of the tree and bent down to knit her fingers together into a stirrup. Kari put her foot on Kasi's hands, and they pushed up together, lifting Kari up to grab onto one branch, then put her other foot onto another branch, and up she went.

However, she didn't get far before she froze, listening.

"What? Are you okay?" Kasi reached up to brace her legs from falling.

Kari shook her head, letting go of her handhold on a branch to put a finger to her lips. She then pointed to her ear.

The voices Kari had heard were getting closer, and she could tell now they were definitely on the other side of the wall.

She wished she was higher up, as her head was just at the level of the top of the wall. But no matter how she strained her neck, she couldn't see over to get a look at who was speaking. She didn't dare climb higher. Not only did her own movements make it hard to hear, but whoever it was might hear and see her.

The most that she could tell was that it sounded like a man and a woman. Though she could only make out a few words and phrases at first, something in the tone made a chill run up her spine. Despite the clandestine location in the back acreage of the Abbey and that they were clearly trying to keep their voices low and not call attention to themselves, the conversation was quickly escalating into an argument.

Chapter 15

Kari

Kari was almost holding her breath as she tried to listen to the argument on the other side of the Abbey wall. She clung tightly to the branches of the old Cypress, although she knew if she stayed in this awkward position halfway up the tree, before long, her legs would start to cramp.

After a minute of jumbled phrases, most of them emphasizing something urgent, like "right now" and "have to do this," she finally started to hear them clearly as the man raised his voice in anger.

"We can't do that, Mandy," the man was saying, "It'll just make it look suspicious."

"No, no, Sam, we have to cover this up. We can't take any risks on them finding out about this or we'll lose our chance."

Sweat from Kari's palms was soaking into the tree bark. Oh no! Were she and Kasi too late? Were they covering up some evidence that was hidden in the back yard right now? Or was it bigger than that? Were they talking about some greater conspiracy to cover up the whole murder case?

Kari was a little afraid she wouldn't be able to hear much more over her own accelerating heartbeat pounding in her ears, but then this time the man, Sam, actually shouted.

"You think I don't know that? None of this would have happened if you had taken the head shot sooner, like I told you to!"

"Oh, it's my fault now? Well, pardon me if I wanted it done professionally! You're the one who hired that amateur to take care of it for us."

"I've had enough of this. You do whatever you want."

"What? Sam, come back here! I can't handle all this by myself!" The rest the argument was drowned out as a small dog started yapping furiously. Both the voices and the barking faded away as if they were heading back towards the condos inside.

Kari was shocked. Had they been planning to shoot someone in the head? Or were they talking about hiring a professional hit man to murder someone? She was so confused and scared that her knees started shaking as she hugged the tree trunk.

She clambered down from the branches and pulled Kasi close. They sat down and huddled on the roots on the far side of the tree, away from the wall that seemed suddenly haunted and foreboding.

"Did you hear all that?" she whispered.

"I think so." Kasi was wide-eyed and white as a sheet. "At first, I was thinking it couldn't be Mandy and Sam Finch, could it?"

"Right, but then I heard the dog. It sounds just like the little dog Rebecca told me about, the one the Finch's own." Kari said.

"Do you think the girl was shot before she fell?"

"I don't know. I don't think so? I mean Hunter didn't say anything about it, but last time we spoke they didn't have the autopsy report back. It kind of sounds like they wanted her shot somewhere secret instead of pushed off the roof, like maybe the amateur didn't kill her the way they wanted, too high profile."

"That's despicable! What could they possibly gain by this?" Kasi asked.

"One thing's for sure, I don't think they had time to cover or bury anything back there before Sam stormed off. We should get in there and look for any evidence, quick."

"Oh, Kari, I don't know if I want to go in there." She nervously tugged at her bottom lip. "What if they come back?"

Kari bit one of her fingernails in her own nervous gesture. "Maybe. We'll just have to play it off. What's our story? Come on let's get up and think." Kari stood and helped her sister to her feet.

"Okay, okay, um," Kasi closed her eyes and took a few deep breaths. "We know Rebecca and Penny. We can say we came to see them."

"That's good. And if they see us around back, we'll say we came outside for a picnic or something." Kari said.

"We don't exactly have a picnic basket and blanket in the car, sis." Kasi countered.

"Of course, but Penny and Rebecca just went inside to get the food. See? Easy!"

"If you say so." Kasi did not look reassured.

The two girls jogged around front, then slowed to a casual walk and tried to look nonchalant as they strolled in the front gate. It was quiet inside the walls of the Abbey except for the swaying trees and birds singing, oblivious to the murder scene's ominous mood. They saw no one as they quickly moved around behind the main building, but everywhere around the building, they saw more crime scene tape.

"Hey, that helps us, actually." Kasi pointed at the taped off areas.

"Oh yeah, you're right, because the cops have already checked all over in those areas." Kari said.

"So any hidden new evidence will be elsewhere. Look," she pointed at the dense landscaping between the outbuilding and the main hall building. "I think there's a path there to get around back."

Kari saw it too, an unpaved trail where the grass was a little thinner from being walked on. The girls went over and followed it between hedges and little rose gardens. They passed through a trellis and found themselves in an open area of grass in the back.

There weren't many hiding places besides under the old trees and stone benches. It didn't take long at all to eliminate any chance of finding a ladder. After half an hour of splitting up and searching, looking over their shoulders every minute for the Finches to return, they hadn't found a bag or a scrap of abandoned clothing. There was nothing to indicate trespassers might have been here.

Kasi stood up from examining a mosaic birdbath, stretching her back as Kari came over to her.

"Anything?" Kari asked.

"Nope. I think this clue-hunting a bust, at least out here." Kasi said.

"Yeah, me too. The most I found was a squeaky toy that Mr. Snappypants left as an offering at the statue of St. Francis."

"Oh, I've seen more than a few of his 'offerings' around here, and not the kind any saint would want. You'd think the Finches would clean up after their dog better knowing other people live here too!"

"Shh! Kasi!" Kari cautioned.

Kasi dropped her voice to a whisper. "Oh right, oops."

"Let's find our way into the main building. We need to check out the roof before it gets dark, and before we start to look suspicious." Kari said.

"I think it's too late for that, sis." Kasi had a doubtful look, but she followed Kari up to the narrow, weathered-brick porch anyway.

The back door of the Abbey was old and ornate, made of thick wood beams with iron hinges. However, it became much less formidable when they realized it was ajar. The Finches must have left it open when they rushed back inside. The girls took advantage, silently agreeing with a look that neither wanted to have to go around front and try to negotiate with any security or staff near the front offices.

Kari led the way towards the stairs, but as soon as Kasi saw the old wood construction, she grabbed her sister's arm.

"There's an elevator right over there. If we go up this way, everybody's going to hear us coming." Kasi said.

Kari shook her head. "The elevator's too old. We could get stuck in there. And besides, it's creepy."

"You've got me there. Great, either we get caught halfway to the roof on the creaky stairs or we have to climb three flights of said stairs to get there." Kasi groused.

"We've got this, sis. Anyone we see, we just tell them we're visiting our friends. Half the people here just come in for the season. They won't even recognize us."

Kasi held out a hand wearily. "Lead on."

Working their way up, they tried to keep close to the wall to make as few creaks as possible, but it didn't do much good. Still, everyone's doors seemed to be closed, and there were plenty of homey sounds from behind them of televisions, music, cooking or chatting people.

"Somebody on the second floor is cooking something yummy." Kasi whispered as they rounded the banister to take the third flight of stairs to the top floor.

"I know, it's making me hungry too," Kari had to admit.

"Promise me you'll take me out for dinner after we're done with this crazy idea."

"Pretty sure this crazy idea was yours, my darling sister."

"Nuh-uh, you were thinking the exact same thing, and you know it." Kasi said.

"Touché. But yeah, definitely dinner after this. Hey, check it out!"

As their heads came above the landing at the end of the stairs, Kari spotted a door at the end of the hall with a sign reading, "Roof Access."

"Score!" Kasi replied, and they both moved forward with renewed enthusiasm. Still, they tried to step as lightly as they could on the old wood floor as they jogged straight for the door. Kari opened it to find yet another set of stairs. This stairwell was a much narrower enclosure, but these steps looked almost new, as did the paneled walls surrounding them.

The sound of a door opening somewhere in the hallways behind them made Kasi squeak in fright. She shoved Kari into the tiny stairwell and shut the door behind them. This made the space suddenly very dim,

but there was just enough light to see the stairs
filtering in from a little skylight over their heads.

"I can see a light bulb hanging up there," Kasi
whispered, "There's a light switch right here."

"No, wait!" Kari hissed, grabbing her hand before she
could flip the switch up. "It might turn on some other
light on the roof. What if somebody's already up
there?"

The weight of her own words sunk into Kari's heart,
and Kasi's face looked much the same as she stared
up at her. Still, Kari turned and lifted her feet, which
felt like chunks of ice, up the stairs one at a time. She
kept hold of her sister's hand, and Kasi did the same,
gripping her fingers tightly.

At the top was a narrow door with no window. She
had figured there would be some kind of warning
signs, something like 'emergency exit: alarm will
sound' or 'maintenance only,' but there was absolutely
nothing on the door. Kari had no idea what to expect.

She grasped the knob and turned it slowly, hoping it
wouldn't squeak or stick. It only made a quiet click,
and she carefully opened the door a crack. Nothing
made a sound on the other side except the wind in
the trees, and she could only see a little sliver of the
evening sky, so she risked opening it a few inches
more to stick her head out.

Kari froze and gaped in shock at what she saw. She felt Kasi push close up behind her, having seen her startled look, and lean in over her shoulder. Kari heard her sister's gasp as she saw it too.

Chapter 16

Kari

Letting go of the doorknob, Kari let the door swing all the way open with the gentle breeze blowing in across the rooftop. The two sisters stepped out of the narrow doorway into an expansive deck that reached half the length of the Abbey rooftop.

It was like they had stepped into a completely different universe. They had left behind the aging bricks, wood and glass, and the historical blend of New England and Old English architecture gently cobbled together with a few modern amenities. Before them was something more like an eclectic café retreat in Sedona or San Francisco.

As they moved forward, the boards under their feet were soon covered by rag rugs woven from what looked like plastic bags and candy wrappers.

All around them were chairs and tables made of reclaimed wood. Some were tall bistro-style furniture, others are reclining Adirondack chairs and stools. Each had words and symbols carved or burned into their flaking paint and fading wood; things like "love" and "joy" as well as peace signs, yin and yang, or complex shapes that Kari thought must be some of the sacred geometry she'd heard about in college.

128

Others just had pop culture characters or cute animal faces.

All the chairs were padded with vividly colored pillows and cushions. Some of these were also made from upcycled t-shirts and jeans, while others were intricately embroidered and covered in sequins and tiny mirrors.

In one corner were some striped umbrellas and stands, but they were folded up and laid flat on the deck, probably because they got more use in the middle of summer. In cooler weather, the residents probably had more use for the half-dozen propane fire columns, around which many of the chairs were circled.

On each handmade table was a planter overflowing with flowers, mums, asters and daisies, and bigger planters lined the deck at the base of the railing, all of them full of trailing vines and lush shrubs as well as taller flowers like goldenrod and sage.

"What. The. Heck. Kasi."

"Right? This is so..."

"Amazing."

"Stunning."

"Gorgeous!"

"Wonderful!"

The two girls clasped hands, this time tickled with joy instead of fear, gaping at each other and then back at the little paradise hidden away on the rooftop of the old building.

"How did we not know about this? Penny and Rebecca have been keeping secrets."

"I honestly don't blame them. I would want to keep this all to myself and my best of friends, too. No wonder Rebecca's so creative with spaces like this to relax in." Kasi looked around at all the decorations, then mused quietly, "I wonder who made these chairs. Maybe we could commission some and put them out in front of the coffee shop. I bet—"

Kari suddenly stopped listening, as a realization washed over her. "Oh, no," she muttered, putting a hand to her mouth.

"What?" Kasi immediately snapped out of her reverie and tensed again. "Did you see something? A clue?"

"No, just the opposite," Kari sighed. "Now that's a perfectly good reason for that girl to be up here. There's so much you could do: stargaze, have a glass of wine and relax by the fire, read, draw, or whatever creative pursuit people here might have. What if she was just checking out the view?" She gestured towards the truly beautiful sunset that was just

130

starting to the west, painting all the rooftops, spires, telephone poles and treetops of Mills Township in a honey gold light.

"Oh, yeah." Kasi frowned, albeit only a little as she, too, looked at the beautiful scene. "Hey, but chances are she probably wasn't up here alone. And she was still dressed in that weird costume for some reason, right?"

"Good point. Let's check it out." Kari nodded resolutely.

It didn't take long to canvas the deck, and check under every chair and table. Kari shook her head when Kasi mentioned a passing thought to dig into the planters a little, maybe for hastily hidden weapons, and Kasi agreed it was silly.

Kari looked at the wood surfaces, both old tables and new decking, and wondered if the police could even pull a fingerprint off them. Hunter would know.

She bit her lip. There was only so much she and her sister could do, and they only had the suspicious conversation to give him right now, but eventually she was going to have to tell him what they were up to.

"Hey, sis, come here!"

131

Kari turned from her musings about Hunter to see Kasi leaning on the railing on the other side of the deck, close to the corner where the girl had fallen.

"Kasi! Be careful!"

Kasi turned and grinned at her. "My point exactly. Come look at this."

Squinting, Kari did so, coming to stand beside her sister and look over the edge of the rail.

"Oh, that's interesting."

Beyond the edge of the deck, there were still several feet of the Abbey's slate roof on all sides, not to mention a raised edge, which was clearly collecting leaves and probably had to be cleaned out regularly. She could see the supports and braces for the deck below them if she leaned over a little. However, the railing was a little higher than on the average backyard deck, up to just under her rib cage, and she couldn't lean out very far without some effort.

Looking at the ground below, from this angle and even on tiptoe, she couldn't see any of the areas that were blocked off with police tape, nothing that was close to the base of the building.

"I don't think anybody could fall from here, not unless they were doing some crazy climbing." Kari said.

"That's what I thought, but I wondered, too…why isn't the railing even higher? Or maybe even fenced in? I would think it would be safer."

"Actually, it makes perfect sense!"

"What does?" Kasi asked.

"That's why we didn't notice this place was up here. It's a historical building, so they try to preserve the look and feel of that when you view it from the street." Kari turned and pointed at the umbrellas folded up on the deck. "That's why the umbrellas are all lying down, and these fire towers are the kind that are less than four feet tall."

"Oh, I get it, secret oasis is secret, so you can't have anything too tall." She looked over the rail again, "And the deck can only be so wide, too. Hence, the few feet of rooftop beyond that sticks out there. So, if someone did fall, they'd just land on the roof. It would have to be quite a jump to make it all the way over the edge." Kasi said.

"That still means the girl must've climbed out there to the edge of the roof before she fell. And if so, how did nobody inside hear someone clomping around out there?"

"Hmm, maybe the people who rent the condo below have already flown south for the season?" Kasi shrugged.

133

"Ugh, that makes sense, too."

"But, why would she even go out there?" Kasi waved an arm out towards the crenelated brickwork at the edge. "A prank?"

"A dare? Some kind of performance art? Just trying to scare somebody? Practicing her edgy parkour gymnastics? I have no idea." Kari covered her mouth with her hand again, another chill gripping her spine. "Oh my gosh, what if her killer carried her out there and threw her off?"

"Geez, Kari! That would be awful." Kasi looked at the roof again. "I don't know, though. That would be hard to do, knock somebody out and haul them over all this? They have to be in really good shape not to get themselves hurt. And then they had to make their getaway right after, otherwise someone would've caught them up here. I'm not sure there's any way to climb back up to the deck once you're down there."

Kari put her hand on her forehead. "You're right, though, there're just too many maybes."

Kasi nodded.

"We have to call Hunter," the two of them said simultaneously.

Chapter 17

Hunter

Hunter stood in the conference room and stared at the murder board. "I'm missing something, and I know it!"

Jo walked into the room and asked, "Talking to that board again?"

"I can't help it. My gut tells me that there's more to this murder investigation than I'm seeing. Moore traveled all the way here from Portland. Her only connection to Mills Township is Damon Greer but according to him, he didn't know she was in town, nor did he recognize her in the nun's costume."

"Well, there's no doubt about it, this one is a tough case," Jo said. "Do you believe Greer?"

"Truthfully it doesn't matter what I believe. It's what I can prove that counts. He definitely has issues with his story and his alibi isn't rock solid. But I have nothing that would tie him to the murder."

Hunter plopped down into a chair in the conference table and stared at the board as if waiting for it to open up and reveal the killer.

Hunter's phone started ringing and he smiled when he saw that it was Kari.

"And on that note, I'll see you later." Jo chuckled as she walked out of the room.

"Hey, Kari. I wasn't expecting to hear from you this afternoon."

The expression on Hunter's face went from happy to serious in seconds as he heard the reason for her call.

"Kasi and I are over at the Abbey we've found something you need to see immediately."

"What are you and Kasi doing out there?" The frustration was evident in Hunter's voice. "Ok, don't do anything else, I'm on my way."

He rushed into the squad room and looked around for one of the junior officers to accompany him. "Flynn!" He shouted. "What are you doing?"

"Nothing sir, just paperwork." The rookie cop jumped up with a mixture of excitement and anxiety.

Johnny Flynn had only been with the department a few months, but already learned that there were only two reasons that Hunter yelled at you...either you screwed up really bad, or he was going to assign you some menial grunt work. Either way, Flynn just knew his day was not going to end well.

"Good, you're coming with me out to the Abbey!"

"Huh?" Flynn looked shocked that he was going to do some actual police work.

"You got something better to do?" Hunter snapped.

"No, sir. "Flynn quickly slid the paperwork he was working on in a folder and placed it in his desk drawer, then hurried to catch up with Hunter.

The silence was thick in the car as they sped to the Abbey. Hunter was frustrated, and it showed. Flynn smartly refrained from asking the senior officer any of the typical rookie questions that usually accompanied being trapped in a car for too long.

Hunter tried to stay calm as he drove. Kari and Kasi are just trying to help, he thought, but it did nothing to curb his concern. No matter how much he told himself that they were in no danger at the moment, Hunter had a hard time convincing his heart.

"It's my fault if something happens to her, I should've never let her come with me the night of the murder," Hunter muttered to himself. "But no, I wanted to keep her with me as long as I could. Now she feels like she needs to get involved."

"I'm sorry, sir. What did you say?" Flynn finally summoned enough courage to break the silence.

"Huh? Oh, nothing. Sorry I'm being so cryptic. We just have two concerned citizens poking their noses into our investigation. No matter how cute her nose is, I can't let her do that. She could end up in a lot of danger."

"Oh, now I see," Flynn said with a smile. "Your girlfriend has got you all riled up. They sure can be a lot of trouble, but, man, they're worth it. Don't be too hard on her, at least she isn't one of those that are always screaming about how dangerous your job is, or who breaks it off with you because they can't handle it."

Although Hunter probably should've corrected Flynn about his and Kari's dating status, he found himself keeping silent. He might want her to be his girlfriend, but truth be told, he had no claims on her.

He knew there was a lot of truth in the rookie's statement. There were a lot of guys in law enforcement who'd had their lives turned upside down because their significant other demanded they choose the job or them.

I want Kari to accept my job; I just don't want her getting involved if she's going to put herself in danger.

As they pulled into the parking lot, Hunter saw the two sisters beside Kari's car. "At least they waited out in the open," he growled to Flynn.

As Hunter exited the car, he kept telling himself not to be too hard on Kari.

"I know Kasi and I shouldn't be here snooping around, but you'll forgive me after you hear what we found out." Kari started to apologize as soon as he was within earshot.

"Girls, I know you're just trying to help, but you really shouldn't be out here doing this," Hunter said, his expression a mixture of fear and anger. "You could've put yourselves in some real danger. What if the murderer was still lurking around?"

"But…" Kari tried to interrupt Hunter, but he continued on as if she hadn't said a word.

"I just don't want to see you two get into any trouble. Or get hurt. This is police business. Please let the professionals handle it, okay?"

Kari threw up her hands, and said, "Okay, Dad. I get it you're worried, but we're big girls and can take care of ourselves. Now, do you want to hear what we found out or not?"

Hunter couldn't help but laugh at Kari's sharp retort. Even Officer Flynn snickered at the brave girl's attitude.

"Well, since we're here I guess you probably should tell Officer Flynn and myself what was so important," Hunter said after he stopped laughing.

With a gleam in her eye, Kari described to the two officers how they were checking out a tree near the back of the property and overheard the Finch's discussing covering up something and wanting to do a headshot but one of them messed it up.

As Kari paused for a breath, Kasi picked up where she left off and described them finding the unexpected rooftop deck and how they surmised that was where the victim fell from.

Once the girls had finished, they stood back and waited for Hunter to say something.

"Now, that is interesting. We saw the deck, of course, but it might warrant a second look. And the conversation that you heard between the husband and wife does sound suspicious. We'll check it out. You two wait here. I don't want you putting yourself in any more danger, okay?"

Both Kari and Kasi reluctantly nodded their heads in agreement.

"Thanks. I don't want to be worried about you two getting into trouble." He winked at Kari as he and Flynn headed toward the entrance to the Abbey.

Hunter found it hard not to tell he girls he was proud of their efforts. The conversation they overhead could be a big break. But he was afraid that if he praised their efforts too much, they would only use it as an excuse to help out more next time.

"Let's check out that rooftop deck before we visit the Finch's. Maybe we'll find something that we can use as leverage." Hunter said to Flynn. "Then we can call on our suspects. I think I'll let you handle the interview this time."

"Really? Thanks!"

"I guess I owe it to you, after the way I snapped at you earlier." Hunter said apologetically.

"Think nothing of it. If the girl I love did the same thing Kari did, I'd be on edge, too."

For a moment, Hunter was taken aback. Is it so obvious that I have such strong feelings for Kari that everyone thinks I'm in love with her? Am I in love with her?

For the time being, Hunter had to push those thoughts to the back of his mind. He was on duty and about to question a potential suspect regarding a murder; he needed to be fully focused. Those were questions he was going to have to entertain later.

Twenty minutes later, Hunter and Officer Flynn exited the door to the Abbey laughing hysterically. As they reached the spot where they had last seen the sisters, they both tried to contain their amusement.

"Well?" Kari asked. "What's so funny?"

Hunter found it hard to answer her with a straight face. "It appears that the covering up you heard was an argument about their dog, Mr. Snappypants."

Once again, both Hunter and Flynn lost it and roared with laughter. Seeing the frustrated looks on both Kari's and Kasi's faces, the amused cops tried to calm down.

"I'm sorry, Kari, it's just so funny. Not you, of course, but a dog named Snappypants!" Hunter choked out between hoots.

"It seems that the headshot they were referring to was for his upcoming advertising debut," Flynn managed to add.

"He's the next face of Chester's Chews!" Hunter doubled up once again in laughter.

"Apparently, 'ol Snappypants got a bad haircut around his tail and they were arguing over how to cover the spot up," Flynn said, his face crimson with suppressed laughter.

"Are you done making fun of us now?" Kari looked peeved.

"Oh, Kari, we're not laughing at you. We really appreciate you two calling with what you found out today." Hunter stopped laughing and looked intently at the two sisters. "You did provide us with a valuable clue. That rooftop deck will need to be checked again by the crime scene unit. You might just have found where our disguised nun was murdered."

"And what about the Finch's?" Kari asked.

Once again, the two cops roared with laughter. "Well, we needed a good laugh today." Hunter said. "Who in the world would name their dog Mr. Snappypants?"

It wasn't long before all four were doubled up with laugher.

After a few minutes, Hunter pulled Kari away from the others. "In all seriousness, Kari. I really appreciate that you wanted to help. But, please don't do something like this again. It scared me when I heard you were out here snooping around, and anything could happen on a murder investigation. I don't know what I'd do if you got hurt. Okay?"

"You don't have to worry about me. I can take care of myself."

Hunter took Kari by the hand and said, "I know you can. But if something happened to you, I would feel like it was my fault. Will you please leave the detective work to me?"

"I'll try," was all Kari was able to promise.

Hunter hugged her. At least it was a start.

Chapter 18

Kari

"Well, that was embarrassing," Kasi said when they climbed back into the jeep. "Were we stupid to think that headshot referred to an actual gunshot in the head rather than a promo photo?"

"No," Kari said with a shake of her head as she pulled out onto the main road. "Think about it: we were there looking for clues to a murder. Of course, our minds would go to bodily harm instead of pooch publicity shots!"

"Yeah, that makes sense," Kasi agreed. "Boy, those two seemed really mad at each other, though! And all over a dog?"

"It's amazing what couples get into fights about," Kari told her.

"Speaking of fights, I thought Hunter was going to blow his top when he first walked up to us!"

"Do you think he's really mad at us?" The thought made Kari a little queasy. She had to admit that their little adventure had been pretty dumb and that they could've compromised the investigation. She wouldn't have blamed Hunter if he was more than a little miffed at them.

Kasi shrugged. "Even if he is, he'll get over it. Come on, you know he can't stay mad at you, big sis."

"Let's hope not. But I don't really want to think about Hunter being mad at me right now. You know what I do want to think about?"

"Eating a lot of carbs?" Kasi said, reading her mind like usual.

"Oh, yeah! How does Taste of Italy sound to you?"

"When has Taste of Italy ever sounded bad to me?" Kasi pointed out. "You know that there's nothing in my world that a loaf of garlic bread and pound of pasta can't cure."

Kari snagged a parking spot directly in front of their favorite Italian restaurant and the two walked in to the welcome smells of marinara and garlic.

"Why don't we just live here?" Kasi asked reasonably. "We could smell these scents every single day."

"Hmm, let's ask the owners if they'll rent out a booth for us to sleep in," Kari said with a laugh as they were led to a table near the back. "That way we can smell garlic all night and coffee all day."

"Sounds like heaven to me." Kasi picked up her menu, then put it back down. "Why do I even look? I have every single dish here memorized and today is definitely a Fettuccine Alfredo day! With maybe some extra parmesan."

Kari was trying to decide between the eggplant parmesan and the shrimp scampi when she saw a familiar face emerge from one of the semi-private back booths in the corner. "Isn't that Penny?" she whispered.

"Oh, hi, guys," Penny said when she saw them at the table, her face a bright pink. "I—uh—was just grabbing a quick bite. Good to see you!" She rushed past them on her way to bathroom.

"Um, that was pretty weird," Kari said when Penny was out of earshot. "That girl is definitely hiding something."

"You think it's something about the dead girl?" Kasi asked, her eyes wide. "I mean, she does live at the Abbey and she never did give a good alibi for what she was doing that night."

"Who do you think is in that booth?" Kari whispered, indicating the back booth that Penny had emerged from. It was one of several with sheer curtains that could be pulled for extra privacy and was usually occupied by new couples or those celebrating an anniversary.

"The curtains aren't totally pulled together, I bet I can see in!" Kasi got up and headed toward the booth, pretending to be interested in the pictures of Sicily that adorned the back wall. After a few moments, she nonchalantly reclaimed her seat at the girls' table.

"Well?" Kari asked.

"It's Paul Dickerson!" Kasi whispered.

Paul Dickerson was an attorney at one of the firms in town that focused on personal injury cases. He was tall, good-looking in a slick sort of way, and a prominent member of the community. He also happened to be very married.

"Isn't he…?" Kasi asked her sister with a raised eyebrow.

"Married? Yes," Kari confirmed.

"Wow. I didn't think Penny was the type to see a married man. I wonder what the story is there?"

When Penny emerged from the bathroom, Kasi beckoned her over. "What are you doing?" Kasi whispered. "You're out in public with a married man!"

Penny just shook her head. "I can't talk about it right now," she told them. "Can I come in and see you guys in the morning?"

148

Before they could answer, Penny rushed back to her booth and pulled the curtains tight.

"Well that wasn't the least bit suspicious," Kari said, suddenly wishing she'd ordered a glass of wine with her dinner instead of her usual tea.

Kasi let out a long sigh. "People make some stupid decisions when it comes to love," she said wisely.

"Oh, really?" Kari couldn't help but smirk. "And what stupid decisions have you made in the name of love? I don't even remember the last relationship you were in."

"Hey, last time I tried... well, you know." Kasi said.

"You're right. I'm sorry."

"No, you're right." Kasi said. "But for now, it's easier to avoid complications by avoiding relationships completely."

Kari unwrapped her silverware and examined it for a few seconds, trying to untangle her thoughts. *Did Penny's behavior mean she's involved with something a lot more serious than an affair?* She wondered. *Or is she just being shifty because she's been caught in the act?*

Both girls were happy when their food arrived a few minutes later and they were able to forego conversation in favor of stuffing their faces. Before too long, though, Kasi put her fork aside and said, "It just doesn't make a whole lot of sense to me."

"What?" Kari asked, swallowing a bit of eggplant. *Yep, wine would definitely have made this better.*

"Penny. I mean, she's young, she's pretty, she's got a good job. Why does she need to sell herself short by seeing a married man?"

Kari shrugged. "People do things for all kinds of reasons, Kasi. We're going to have to ask her when she comes in tomorrow."

"She was always one of the most popular girls in high school," Kasi continued as if she hadn't heard a word her sister had said. "On the cheerleader squad, dated a lot of the football players...she could have anyone she'd wanted."

"Things sometimes look a lot different from the outside looking in."

"And what about Paul? What a snake!" Kasi was really up in arms now. She had her bread knife clenched in one hand and was waving it around to make a point. "You see him around town holding hands with his wife all the time! And don't they have a little girl in kindergarten? Sheesh! The next time he comes into the shop, I'm gonna spike his coffee with a laxative!"

Kari couldn't help it. She snorted out a laugh that attracted the attention of several nearby diners.

"What?" Kasi asked innocently. "Come on, you can't tell me it doesn't upset you, too."

"It does," Kari confirmed, "But it's not really my business. My many years of wisdom have shown me that getting upset about how others act is just a recipe for disaster."

"Ohhh, of course, you have so many more years of wisdom than I do." Kasi had a smile on her face, but there was an edge to her words. She'd always been less forgiving of others than her sister and expected a certain code of conduct from people—especially those she considered friends.

Knowing this about her sister, Kari gently pointed out, "And Penny's at fault too, you know. It takes…two to tango." She cringed at her own cliché but didn't know how else to put it delicately.

"Oh, I'm not letting her off the hook," Kasi assured her. "You know what? I don't want to be here when the two of them make their separate exits and try to act all innocent. What do you think about getting our dessert to go?"

Kari thought about sharing a big helping of tiramisu with her sister as they lounged in their pajamas and caught some late-night TV. Nothing had sounded that appealing to her in a long time. "I think that's perfect," she told her.

Kasi nodded and signaled the waitress. "Good. Then we can talk in private about what we should say to Penny when she comes in tomorrow."

Kari told her it sounded like a good plan and they began gathering their things to leave.

Until tomorrow, Kari silently told the curtained booth. *You'd better be prepared for the third degree, Penny. When the Sweet sisters have questions, you'd better bet we get answers.*

Chapter 19

Kari

It was around eight o'clock in the morning, just as the breakfast rush was dying down, and customers had grabbed all their to-go orders before work that Kari saw Penny Green again.

She took a moment to give the cappuccino machine a break while she walked over to the front window, raising the shade from halfway down to completely open now that the sun was a little higher in the sky. Just as she was finishing up, she spotted Penny through the window, walking down the street towards the coffee shop.

She rushed back behind the counter and nudged Kasi with her elbow.

"She's here!"

"Who?" Kasi looked up from slicing a freshly toasted croissant. Kari waggled her eyebrows suggestively, and Kasi said, "Oh! Wow, she didn't chicken out this time?"

"Apparently not." Kari nodded towards the door as it opened, the little bell rang brightly as Penny entered and came to stand at the end of the relatively short line. She was standing with her hands clenching the handles of her bag and looking around the room nervously where some of the retired patrons were still enjoying their morning newspapers and crossword puzzles.

When she reached the register, both girls were standing side-by-side, looking at her expectantly.

"Um...I'll—ah...just a black coffee, please."

"For here?" Kasi asked in a snippy tone, tipping her head to the side. Kari kicked her behind the counter, but she pretended not to notice.

Penny sighed, smiling and blushing, and Kari was reminded of her in school whenever one of the sisters caught their friend doing something childish. "Yes, I promise I won't run away again."

Once they had poured some rich-smelling French Roast in a mug for her, the three of them sat on a table a little away from the other customers, and Penny started to talk.

"I almost came over here before you were even open, but I wasn't sure what time you get here in the morning, or even that you'd let me in. But then I realized I was just avoiding the problem even more by trying to keep anyone from overhearing. Besides, Paul and I have been in and out of every restaurant in the nearest six towns! Somebody else has to have seen us by now."

"You're lucky I'm not as indiscreet as the gossips around here. Otherwise the rumor mill could have ground you to a pulp before you even knew it."

"Kasi!"

"What? It's true."

"No, no, Kari, she's right. I needed a reality check. But to tell you the truth, it wasn't seeing you that was the real bucket of ice water in my face."

"Oh really, what was it?"

Penny sat down heavily at one of the tables, folding her hands in her lap and looking at the floor. "I've actually been avoiding going to the police to give my statement about the night that woman died at the Abbey."

Both Kari and Kasi covered their mouths in surprise, giving each other looks of horror. Penny went on without waiting for their response, without even looking up at them.

"Paul was with me in my condo that afternoon. He told his wife he had a meeting that was running late just so he could come see me. It seemed so spontaneous at the time, but then all the screams and commotion started up."

"I had to tell him to hide in my shower while I went outside to see what the matter was. I was so scared the cops would search the building and find him. And then I found out that the girl had been murdered, and that anyone in the building could be a suspect. But, of course, I had an alibi, and...well..."

"And what?"

"We have photos on our phones proving we were together at the time she fell."

"Oh! Okay, enough said." Kari was sure her face was turning just as pink as Kasi's was.

Penny put her face in her hands. "I'm so embarrassed. I never thought anyone would know about me and Paul. It's made all the difference thinking of having to tell someone I knew in high school, like Officer Houston, or seeing Officer Kingston's disapproving look."

Kari winced in sympathy. "I think their disapproval would deter anybody. Still, you're going to have to give your statement eventually."

Kasi came out from behind the counter and sat down next to Penny, her disapproval seeming to have softened a little. "I just don't understand why you would do all this, sweetie. You were always the overachiever in school, going out for both drama club and cheerleading, making good grades. You've got brains, talent, and beauty going for you. Why risk your reputation to run around with Paul? Are you really in love?"

Penny looked up, tears shining in her eyes. "That's just it, we're not. At least, well, I'm not. I haven't really talked to him about it." She threw up her hands in frustration. "I just thought it would be something fun, something casual, like dating in high school used to be. Like we used to sneak around behind our parents' backs and kiss when no one was looking. I never thought of it as serious. Now that I think about it, I didn't expect it to go on as long as it has. It was stupid to keep telling myself that's all it was. I guess I'm going to have to grow up and get serious about finding a relationship."

"Not necessarily." Kasi shrugged, "You just have to be honest with yourself and whoever you're dating. There's no law that says you have to settle down and get married." She put her hands on her hips. "Just don't go messing around with men who are married!"

Penny swiped at her eyes with the back of her hand, and Kari reached over to hand her a napkin. She then sat up a little straighter, looking each of the sisters in the eye in turn. "You know what, that's absolutely true. I deserve an honest relationship, and so does his family. I didn't think about who I was hurting, and I should have. I was so wrong."

Kasi reached over and squeezed her shoulder, but then she made a face. "And you're still going to have to tell the cops about this."

Penny chuckled even as she pressed the napkin over her eyes again. "Yeah, I know."

"You can count on the MTPD to be discreet." Kari assured her with a smile. "I'm sure Hunter wouldn't even make you show him the photos. He'll take your word for it." Silently in her own mind she added, *he better not be looking at those photos, or I'll have something to say about it. If somebody has to look, he better have Jo do it.*

"That's right." Kasi added, "All they really want to know is who killed that poor girl and why."

Penny nodded. "I wish I could help with that. I don't think my statement will help at all. I was more than a little distracted and didn't see anyone or anything suspicious." She looked sheepish as she twisted her purse handles between her hands.

"Why don't you go over to the station right now?" Kari suggested. "I'm sure your work will understand if you're a little late, what with all the stressful stuff going on around the Abbey murder. Here, I'll even call Hunter and let him know you're coming. He'll be ready to go when you get there, and you won't even have to wait at the station for long."

"You really think so?" Penny stood up from the table, wringing the straps of her purse even more.

Kasi patted her on the back. "You'll feel better after it's all over with."

"You're probably right," Penny sighed. "Okay, then. I'll go now. And thank you for listening, both of you."

"Any time," the two sisters said together. They then gave each other a look of relief as Penny turned and walked out the door.

"You just wanted an excuse to talk to Hunter," Kasi teased as Kari whipped out her phone.

"And you want an update on the case as much as I do," Kari shot back, sticking out her tongue as she listened to the phone ring.

Hunter's voice came through the line, "Well, good morning! I thought it would be at least twenty-four hours before you and your sister got in trouble again."

Rolling her eyes, Kari retorted, "Trouble is starting to follow us around. But seriously, we just talked to Penny Green."

"Really? We've been trying to get in touch with her since the murder."

"Everything's okay, and she's on her way to talk to you."

"Alright, I'll clear some space in the schedule. Anything else?"

"No. Do you have anything else, hint hint?"

"You never give up, do you?"

"Would you want it any other way?"

"Ah..." he hesitated, putting on a skeptical tone, "it does come in handy at times. Anyway, if you must know, we do have an ID on the victim now."

"Really? Who?"

"Her name is Kelsey Moore, an actress from out of state. We know she was visiting a friend here but not much else. The medical examiner just told me that he thinks she was drugged, but toxicology hasn't come back to determine exactly what it was yet, so he won't tell me more. Does that satisfy the cat's curiosity for now?"

"Not quite. You're not getting away from me that easy, Officer Houston. Don't you have any new suspects with all of this?"

"Er...not yet. But there are a couple with distinct holes in their alibis."

"Ooo, tell me more."

"Don't you have a coffee shop to run?"

As if he had summoned them, three more customers walked in the door. Kari knew the detective's keen ears could probably hear the bell over the phone.

"Okay, okay, you got me this time, Houston. But I'll be back."

"Oh, I'm counting on it, Miss Sweet." She could hear him chuckling just before he hung up the phone. The tone of his voice and sound of his laughter sent a little tingle down her spine.

All this time, Kasi had been hovering near the phone. She wasn't quite leaning on Kari's shoulder, but definitely invading her personal space. Kari shooed her towards the cash register, where the fresh batch of customers were staring upward, perusing the menu board.

Kari casually absorbed her sister's piercing gaze as she went through the process of crafting three perfect lattes and two breakfast sandwiches. When the customers were settling down with their respective orders, Kasi poked her in the shoulder.

"You took your sweet time."

"I can't help it. I'm Sweet all the time." Kari retorted.

"Yeah me too, but I won't be if you don't tell me what Hunter said."

"Kelsey Moore." Kari said.

Kasi perked up, all her anger melting away. "They found out who she was? That's great! But I don't know the name."

"That's because she's not from here. You think I'm bad, Hunter wouldn't tell me much, either. She's an actress and came to visit, but that's all he said. However," she held up one finger, "he did tell me that they think she was drugged."

Kasi held out her hands, gaping, "Of course! That makes so much more sense why she could have fallen from the roof deck. She could have been dizzy, or nauseous. Or, wow, do you think she was hallucinating?"

"That's a possibility. Or, if she didn't just fall, she may have been too weak to fight off someone who tried to attack her. Heck, maybe she was trying to get away from someone, but she was so out of it that she forgot she was on a roof?"

Kasi gasped again, her eyes going wide, "You don't think she was on a date with some sleazy guy who tried to make her do something she didn't want to? Geez, that makes Penny's situation look tame in comparison."

"I know! It's scary to think there might be someone that horrible living in our hometown."

Kasi closed her eyes, then snapped her fingers. "Darn it."

"What?"

"That still doesn't explain why she was wearing that nun costume."

The two sisters stared at each other, their brows furrowing. Neither one could think of any explanation for this strange piece of the puzzle.

Chapter 20

Kari

It was Sunday morning and the only day of the week that the Sweet sisters did not open the coffee shop. They had both questioned the wisdom of this since they knew they were missing out on the church crowd that would likely bring in tons of revenue. However, they also knew that if they didn't take at least one day off, they'd likely burn out.

It was already tough on them to handle the shop alone six days a week. Kari remembered early on when her sister had come down with the flu for almost a week, and Kari had nearly had a nervous breakdown trying to run things by herself. In those days, however, they had not been able to afford any help and they'd just had to deal with it.

"I really think we need to revisit the idea of hiring some help," Kari told her sister as they lounged in their pajamas over a pan of cinnamon rolls and some Vienna roast in the kitchen.

Kasi nodded sleepily and covered a big yawn with her hand. "I think you might be right. I know we were concerned before about how much we'd have to pay them, but I think we're in a place now where it makes sense."

"What do you think about hiring a couple of high school students? They've got a great Home Economics program here and I'm sure we could find a couple of girls—or guys—who want to learn more about the service industry."

Kasi considered this for a moment as she chewed a big mouthful of gooey roll. "I like it," she said after swallowing. "They could take some afternoon shifts and weekend shifts and give at least one of us a break. And we could start them at minimum wage."

"Yep, just what I was thinking. Let's put a flier up in the shop tomorrow and maybe put an ad in the paper this week?"

The girls chatted a bit more about their perfect employees as they cleaned up breakfast and got ready for their day. Kari was just finishing up her minimal makeup routine when she heard the doorbell ring.

Her first thought was that Hunter had some more details on the case and she rushed to the door with her heart pounding. It wasn't, however, the town's hunkiest police officer at the door.

"Oh, hi, Penny," Kari greeted her when she saw her in the doorway. "What's up?"

"Penny?" Kasi called over her shoulder, joining her sister at the door. "You okay?"

Penny nodded, though the look on her face told a different story. She looked like she hadn't slept a wink and her blonde hair was thrown back in a messy ponytail. Even her clothes look rumpled, almost as if she'd slept in them. "Can I come in?"

"Oh, of course!" Kari opened the door wider and Kasi led her friend to the couch. "Do you want some coffee?"

"Yes, please," Penny said gratefully, sitting down next to Kari.

"I just brewed some!" Kari hurried into the kitchen and poured Penny a cup, mixing it with half and half. After a second's consideration, she plopped the last cinnamon roll on a plate, then carried both back to the living room.

"What happened?" Kasi asked when Kari joined them.

Penny took the plate and coffee cup, looked at them for a moment, then set them on the table as she burst out in tears.

"Penny!" Kasi put an arm around her. "It's okay, just let it out."

Penny covered her face, her shoulders shaking. After a minute, she got herself together and took a big, shuddering breath. "I've made the decision to break it off with Paul."

Kasi met Kari's eyes, then gave her friend a supportive squeeze. "Good for you, Penny. I know it can't be easy."

Penny wiped her face, then sat up a little straighter. "To be honest, I knew it was a mistake from the beginning. I just got wrapped up in the...whole glamour of the thing, you know? Paul kept telling me how much his wife never even spoke to him anymore but that he couldn't abandon her because she needed his paycheck. He made me feel like I was this ray of light, that I had totally made him believe in love again." She laughed mirthlessly. "What a load of hooey."

"Everyone makes mistakes," Kari assured her while Kasi patted her back. "You can't beat yourself up over it."

"Well, I see the reality of the whole situation now," Penny continued. "Talking to Hunter made me realize how stupid I was being. I could have really gotten myself into a lot of trouble! But I'm determined to end it now. I'm done."

Kasi looked at her sister, and it was clear they were thinking the same thing. What's this got to do with us?

Penny leaned down and rummaged through her purse, producing an envelope. "I've always been better getting my feelings out in writing. So, instead of doing it in person, I decided to break up with him in a letter."

"Good idea," Kasi told her. "That way he can't try to convince you otherwise."

"Exactly. But I have to admit, I'm a little nervous about giving it to him." She looked at each sister in turn, a pleading look on her face. "I was hoping you guys could go with me to deliver it? You know, as moral support?"

"Of course," Kasi said quickly before her sister could protest. "You bet we will."

Penny's shoulders sagged in relief. "Oh, thank goodness! That's such a relief. He's fishing at the lake today, so I thought that would be a good place to do it. He should be relaxed and in a good mood, and, hopefully, won't freak out."

If she's driving to a remote place to dump someone, she does need us, Kari thought. *That just sounds like a recipe for disaster.*

"Just give us a few minutes to get our things together," Kasi told her. "We'll get this over with so you can get on with your life, okay?"

"Thank you again," Penny said, picking up her plate and eyeing the roll. "This looks delish, by the way. Just what the doctor ordered."

"What do you think?" Kasi whispered when the girls were in their bedroom under the pretense of finding their jackets.

"I think he might throw her in the lake, so it's a darn good thing she asked us to go with her," Kari replied.

Kasi nodded. "Exactly what I was thinking. You know, a few months ago, I never would have automatically assumed someone was in danger in this situation. Do you think all this sleuthing is affecting how we look at the world?"

Kari had thought these exact same things recently. "Maybe it was time we stopped being so naïve," she pointed out. "Unfortunately, there's a lot of bad people no matter where you go, and it's only smart to realize that and take the right precautions."

"Yep, I think you're right." Kasi tossed her sister a white Columbia fleece and slipped on her matching purple top. "Now let's go help Penny dump that sleaze."

"I just can't thank you girls enough," Penny said when they were all in her jeep and headed to the lake a few minutes out of town. "I'm so nervous. I thought about just putting it in his mailbox, but what if his wife got it? I knew I had to give it to him in person."

The sisters assured her they were happy to help and that they were glad she hadn't come out to the lake alone.

As they approached the lake entrance that Penny pointed out to them, Kari saw something in the distance that caught her eye. "Oh my gosh, what's that?"

The three women squinted as they tried to focus on a figure that was standing at the bank of the lake. He appeared to be throwing something into the water.

"Get closer!" Kasi hissed.

Kari hurriedly pulled the jeep to the side of the road. "He might hear the engine," she said. "Let's try to get closer on foot!"

They got out of the Jeep and started toward the person, trying to stick close to the trees that lined the side of the road.

"He's leaving!" Kasi whispered.

And that's when they saw it. Oh my gosh, Kari thought. I totally know who that is—and what he might be throwing into the lake.

Chapter 21

Hunter

Hunter wanted coffee. No, scratch that, Hunter
needed coffee. He had been working night and day on
the fake nun case and, even when he wasn't at the
station or out interviewing witnesses, he was still
thinking about it 24/7.

Why had no one come forward to report Kelsey
missing? And who would want to hurt a young girl
like her? There seemed to be more questions than
answers in this case, and it was seriously starting to
mess with his head.

Fortunately, needing coffee dovetailed nicely with the
other thing he needed at the moment—to see Kari
Sweet's beautiful face. Along with thinking
obsessively about the case, he also couldn't stop
thinking about how their date had been ruined by the
same case.

That's the life of a police officer, he kept telling himself. *If
we're going to get involved, she's going to have to get used to it.*

He had to be honest with himself and admit that one
of the reasons he'd never had a serious relationship
was because of his job. He just didn't see how long
and erratic hours would mix with putting someone

else first, so he'd just naturally shied away from getting close to anyone.

Things were different now, though. No matter how hard he tried to keep Kari at a distance, he just felt himself getting closer and closer to her.

He was surprised to find a parking space across from the front doors of On Bitter Ground. Since the murder, the coffee shop had been packed to capacity nearly every time he'd stopped by. While he was happy for the sisters' success, he got a little impatient when he had to stand in line for fifteen minutes to get his caffeine and a smile from his favorite barista. She was worth it, but he was so short on time as of late.

As he entered the shop, Hunter saw that there was indeed a line that he'd not been able to spot from the street. However, his five-minute wait gave him a chance to watch Kari in action and it was certainly a sight to behold.

Kari moved fluidly from the coffee machines to the counter, helping her customers with a warm smile and plenty of kind words. Today, her curly hair was pulled into a French braid that was already starting to come undone, and her bright pink apron covered snug jeans and a long-sleeved white tee shirt. Diamond studs winked in her ears and caught the light as she moved.

She was in, in a word, adorable.

Not only that, but she was admirable, too. He'd long known that both she and her sister were good businesswomen, but he hadn't known the extent of it until he'd gotten to know her better. Everyone he talked to about Kari had something complimentary to say about her and her shop and he felt a wave of pride that this may someday be his girlfriend.

At the mere thought of that, Hunter felt his heart speed up. *Jeez, dude*, he chided himself. *Are you back in high school or what?*

As Hunter struggled to regain control of his hormones, Kari caught a glimpse of him and shot him a big smile. This, of course, just made his heart pound harder.

"Well, how's my favorite customer?" Kari asked when he approached the counter.

"What?" said an elderly man who was waiting for his specialty drink. "I thought I was your favorite!" He gave Kari his best droopy frown, which made him look like a hound dog.

"Oh, don't worry, Mr. Abernathy," Kasi said, handing the man a steaming mug of cappuccino. "You're my favorite. In fact, I like you so much that I'm going to throw in a free piece of biscotti from our good friends over at Playing with Flour." She put the pastry on a small plate and handed it to him with a flourish. "There you are, kind sir!"

173

Hunter smiled at the scene. The girls really were popular with their customers. No wonder their shop had become so successful. "Had to come in and see the prettiest barista in town," he told Kari. "And get my daily fix of caffeine, of course."

"Oh, you came in just to see little old me?" Kasi batted her eyelashes at him. "Oooh, but I think my sister might get jealous!"

Kari swatted at her and started to fill a tall cup with Hunter's favorite brew. "I'm really glad you stopped by. So…how is the case going?"

Hunter couldn't help but chuckle. *I don't know what I was thinking when I was worried about whether Kari would be able to handle my cop's lifestyle*, he thought. *Sometimes I think she's more into it than I am.*

"Well, I think we finally have a few answers," he told her.

"Hmmm, and what are those?" Kasi was directly behind her sister and clearly wasn't going anywhere.

I've really met my match with these two, he thought. *Good thing they're on my side.* "Well, I first want to tell you I appreciate you encouraging Penny to talk to me. I'm happy to report she's been cleared."

"Of the murder, right?" Kasi asked. "Because we all agree she's guilty of poor judgment. Sorry, that's harsh, but adultery is wrong."

"Well, that's a personal matter," Hunter said, "but I'm able to say she's one hundred percent innocent of any crime that would concern the police department."

"What about Paul?" Kari asked. "He seems a little…shady to me."

"A little?" Kasi scoffed. "The man is married with a kid and he's going around seducing my friends! I would say that's a bit more than shady."

"Shady or not, he's been cleared as well. There's no connection whatsoever between him and Kelsey's death."

"Well, at least he has that going for him," Kasi muttered.

Hunter looked behind him to see that a line of customers had formed. The next thing he wanted to tell them he knew shouldn't be discussed in public. "Hey, can we go in the back room for a minute?"

Kasi wiggled her eyebrows. "Hey, Romeo, we've got work to do. What kind of business do you think we're running?"

Kari swatted her again. "Can you handle things for a few while I talk to Hunter?"

"Sure, but you owe me!" Kasi pushed her out of the way, so she could take her place at the counter. Studiously ignoring Hunter, she looked at the next customer in line. "May I help you?"

"What's up?" Kari asked when they stepped into the storage room.

"Well, we got the M.E.'s report," Hunter told her, leaning against the wall. "I didn't think all your customers needed to hear what the cause of death was."

"Oh, good thinking," Kari said with a nod, then looked at him expectantly. "Well? What was it?"

"She had a broken neck, which we pretty much guessed from the position of the body. But cyanide was also found in her bloodstream. The M.E. thinks she was poisoned about 15 minutes before she fell. That would've been enough time for the poison to do its damage. We think she was dead before she hit the ground."

Kari processed this for a moment before she nodded thoughtfully. "Wow, okay. That changes things a bit, doesn't it?"

Hunter watched as she processed the information, then saw her face change. "What is it?" he asked.

"Well, we've got some information for you, too." She quickly told him about their trip to the lake and how they had seen a person throwing something into it. "We went over there after he left to see if we could find out anything else. He couldn't get close enough to the water, so it ended up in the mud by the bank."

"What did?" Hunted demanded, aware that Kari had, once again, put herself in danger without so much as a second thought. He didn't know whether to be grateful for the added information on the case, or furious that she kept butting in.

Kari dug around her pocket before producing a gold ring with a small diamond in it. "This!" she said triumphantly, dropping it into his palm. "But that's not all!"

Hunter waited for a few seconds. "What? Come on, Kari, just tell me what you know."

She looked a little hurt at his impatience but recovered quickly. "Well, the person who threw the ring… He was on crutches."

Hunter gripped the ring tightly in his palm and knew everything was coming together. With this new information he knew that someone needed another visit from the cops.

Chapter 22

Kari

"Well, I feel like we actually helped this time," Kasi said when Hunter left.

"Yeah, unlike the Mr. Snappypants debacle," Kari added with a shake of her head. "I still can't believe we mistook a photo shoot for a murder."

Kasi giggled, then slapped a hand over her mouth. "Sorry! I'm sorry. But you have to admit, it's kind of funny."

"Maybe I'll be able to find it funny down the road," Kari said. "Right now, I still feel like Hunter thinks I'm an idiot."

"Oh, sis, you know he doesn't." Kasi put a comforting arm around her shoulders. "You think he's never made a mistake in a case before? It could've happened to anyone."

"Well, I still feel like I have to prove that we can be valuable assets," Kari told her, pulling out her phone. "You think we can find out anything else about Damon Greer?"

There's no one else in this town that I've seen on crutches. It had to be Damon who tried to throw the ring into the lake.

Kasi served the last customer in the shop her cappuccino and leaned against the counter to see what her sister had found. "You really think Damon is our guy?"

Kari shrugged, scrolling through the results she'd pulled up. "You have to admit throwing a ring into the lake is pretty suspicious," she said. "Whoa, look at this!" She handed the phone to her sister.

"Is that him and…the dead girl?" Kasi asked, her eyes wide. "Oh my gosh…they look pretty cozy!"

Kari took the phone back and scrolled a bit more. "It says they were in a few shows together back in Portland." She looked up at her sister. "Why did we not know this? Look how easy it was for us to find! Do you think Hunter knows?"

"I don't know, but we'd better tell him."

Kari nodded and quickly dialed Hunter's number. When he answered, she hurriedly explained to him about the pictures and the connection between Damon and Kelsey. She listened for a minute, then said, "Yeah, okay. You bet."

"Well??" Kasi demanded when she hung up. "What did he say?"

Kari sighed and sagged against the counter. "They already knew all about this." *And Hunter didn't bother telling me*, she added to herself.

"What do you mean?" Kasi demanded. "What exactly did he say?"

"He said that they found these pictures and realized there was a connection, but that they couldn't get a hold of Kelsey's parents to ask them more about Damon because they were on a mission trip. Apparently, they're really active members of their church."

"So, why didn't he tell us?" Kari pushed.

"He said that they couldn't release the information until they talked to Kelsey's parents." *And he probably didn't want me butting in and messing things up again. I can't say I blame him.*

"Oh." Kasi looked a little deflated. "Well, that makes sense, right? I mean, we aren't actually on the police force."

Kari nodded. She knew she shouldn't be hurt that Hunter had kept the information from her, but she couldn't help herself. As the girls helped the few straggling customers that came in the door and were kept busy with internet orders, she did her best to get over the feeling that Hunter didn't trust her.

When her phone rang a few hours later, her heart sped up when she saw it was Hunter on the line. "Hunter? What is it?" She listened again, her eyes getting wide.

"Oh my gosh, I wish you'd just put him on speaker!" Kasi muttered as she listened to the one-sided conversation. "What now?" she demanded as soon as her sister hung up.

Kari's eyes were once again bright with excitement. "As luck would have it, the parents just got back into town, so they were able to talk to them. It appears that Kelsey was in town to audition for the part of a nun in a historical movie."

"They were shooting a movie here?" Kasi asked. "I hadn't heard anything about that!"

"Me, neither. But I guess it could've been hush-hush. You know how directors don't like their set getting mobbed by a bunch of looky-loos." Kari said.

"I guess so. You'd think we would've heard something, though."

"So, get this, Hunter is going to talk to Damon again. And guess who he invited to come with him?"

Kasi looked at her sister's broad grin. "From your expression, I'm going to guess it isn't me he invited. Don't worry, I'll hold down the fort." She swiped at the counter with her dish towel. "As usual."

"You're the best!" Kari knew her sister wasn't wild about being left out of the adventure, but she was too excited to spend much time dwelling on Kasi's feelings. Kari knew she would make it up to Kasi later, and she knew Kasi would want her to go.

This means Hunter really does value my help! She thought euphorically. *He doesn't think I'm just a pain in the butt who keeps getting in the middle of things!*

Twenty minutes later, Hunter and Kari arrived at the Abbey.

"You sure you're okay doing this?" Hunter asked as he pulled his cruiser to a stop in front of the main building.

"Absolutely!" Kari exclaimed, nearly bouncing out of her seat.

"Just stay behind me at all times, okay?" Hunter told her. "And stay close. No matter what happens, I want you to stick right by my side, okay? And just follow my lead."

"Yep, got it!" She would've agreed to just about anything he asked of her at that moment if it meant she could help him question Damon.

The two arrived at his aunt's door and Hunter knocked loudly. "Ms. Greer?" Hunter called out when no one answered his knock. "It's officer Houston from the Mills Township police department." He glanced at Kari when there was no answer.

"Prudence?" Kari called out. "It's Kari Sweet. Are you home?"

Hunter knocked again, then stepped back when he heard someone shuffling to the door. He put back a protective arm, ensuring that Kari was safely behind him.

"Oh, hello there," Prudence said when she opened the door and saw them. "I'm sorry, have you been here long? I didn't have my hearing aids in. I'm deaf as can be without these little babies." She tapped her ear and smiled at them. "What can I do for you?"

"We're here to see your nephew, ma'am," Hunter told her. "Is he home?"

Prudence shook her head slowly, causing Kari's heart to drop. "No. No, the last I knew, he was going up stairs to visit that artist gal. Renee? No, Rebecca." She smiled triumphantly. "Yes, it's Rebecca!"

Kari looked at Hunter, her eyes wide. "We need to get up there! Fast!" she said. She couldn't help but feel that her friend might be in grave danger.

"Thank you, ma'am," Hunter hurriedly told Prudence before radioing for backup.

"I'll knock on the door and try to draw her out," Kari said as they rushed up the stairs to Rebecca's apartment. "That way, if Damon is in there, he won't realize the police are on to him."

"I don't like the idea of sending you to the door alone, but I think that's probably a solid idea," Hunter conceded. "I'll be right around the corner and have my eyes on you at all times, okay? No matter what you do, do not enter that apartment alone. You understand me?"

Kari nodded as they approached Rebecca's door and Hunter ducked around the corner. "Rebecca?" she called as she knocked. "It's Kari! I wanted to stop by and see if you had some ideas for next week's specials sign!"

After a moment, the door opened and Rebecca peered out of her door, a strained smile on her face. "Uh, hi, Kari."

It was obvious that Rebecca was not acting like herself and Kari knew she had to get her out of her apartment as quickly as possible. "Do you mind coming down to my car to look at the sign? Kasi and I sketched up some ideas, but we definitely need your help!"

"Um, maybe later?" Rebecca said. "I'm really tired right now. Migraine." She shook her head tightly and mouthed some words Kari could not make out.

"Oh well, just a quick look? You don't actually have to do the work right now." Kari was wracking her brain to find a way to get Rebecca out into the hall and out of danger. "We just really need to know if our idea will work or not." Before she could think twice, she reached into the apartment and put her hand on Rebecca's arm. "Come on, I just need you for a sec!"

"Oh no, I don't think you do." The voice belonged to Damon Greer, who had materialized behind Rebecca with a big, nasty smile—and an even nastier knife.

Chapter 23

Hunter

"Kari! Get back!" Hunter yelled as he stepped out from his hiding place.

As soon as Damon saw him, he grabbed Rebecca by the hair and yanked her back into the apartment, pressing the knife close to her neck.

Instinctively, Hunter stepped in front of Kari to put himself in between her and whatever Damon planned to do with the knife.

"Stay away from me or she dies!" Damon spit out in anger.

"Don't do anything you'll regret later. You know you're not getting out of here so why you don't put the knife down before you hurt another innocent girl?"

Keep them calm. That's what all the courses on hostage situations tell you, keep them calm. They forgot to tell me exactly how to keep calm on my first one! Hunter thought to himself.

"What innocent girl?" Damon demanded. "You can't mean Kelsey? She wasn't innocent, she played me for a fool, but I showed her! And I'll show you, too!"

Damon pointed the knife at Hunter to emphasize his point.

A split second before she lashed out at Damon, Hunter saw Rebecca's eyes and recognized the fight-or-flight look just before a terrified person reacts. Much to Hunter's satisfaction, Rebecca chose to fight.

With the knife safely pointed away from her neck, Rebecca grabbed Damon's wrist with both hands to keep him from stabbing her. At the same time, she lifted her leg as high as she could and slammed it into the surgically reconstructed ankle her attacker had favored since she had known him.

Immediately, Damon screamed in pain and dropped to the floor.

Hunter ran into the room kicking the knife away from Damon and rolling him onto his back to handcuff him.

Once his suspect was safely restrained—and still screaming in pain—Hunter ran over to check on Rebecca and Kari. "Are you two alright? He didn't cut you anywhere, did he?"

"No, I'm fine," Rebecca said shakily. "Just shook up. I can't believe Damon tried to kill me!" She collapsed on the floor. "My knees are shaking so bad I don't think I can stand."

"Here, let us help you." Kari took Rebecca's arm, and with Hunter's help, they assisted her over to the couch where she collapsed.

As Kari sat down next to her friend, Hunter took out his cellphone and called Officer Jo Kingston.

"Jo, it's Houston. I'm over at the Abbey and I have Damon Greer in custody. He attacked Rebecca Trang tonight. Oh, and you'd better send over the paramedics. Mr. Greer was injured in the process."

He listened as Jo asked if he had been the one to hurt him.

"No, I didn't touch him. Ms. Trang kicked him in the ankle. "But I sure would've liked to have been the one to take him down! The man threatened my girl. Yep, that ankle," he said when Jo asked with a snort if it had been his injured leg. "I'll tell you all about it when I see you."

Hunter hung up the phone and turned back to Kari and Rebecca. As he walked by Damon, the cuffed man cried out in agony. "I think she broke my leg! You've got to help me."

"The paramedics are on their way," he told the killer coldly. "Until they get here you're just going to have to suffer."

For the next few minutes, Rebecca, Kari and Hunter sat in silence watching Damon writhe on the floor in pain. Each of the girls asked if there was something that could be done for Damon before the ambulance arrived, Hunter wouldn't allow it.

"I find it pretty remarkable that you ladies still have some compassion for that scumbag," he said, unable to hide his disgust. "Unfortunately for him, my hands are tied. The department doesn't allow us to administer any type of medication unless it is in a life-threatening situation. We're just going to have to listen to him until they get here. It shouldn't be long now."

Just then, the sound of sirens could be heard in the distance. "See, I told you."

A few moments later, Jo Kingston and two paramedics came to the still open door of Rebecca's apartment. Once they had Greer stabilized, they placed him on a gurney and turned to exam Rebecca.

"I'm fine, he didn't hurt me," Rebecca said to the paramedic that was inspecting her neck and arm for minor cuts.

"You seem fine physically to me," the paramedic stated. "But in situations like this, it's best to remember that emotionally, you'll likely need some support. You've been through a very traumatic experience and you're still in shock. Do you have someone you can call if you find you're having some trouble later?"

"She can call me or my sister," Kari quickly volunteered.

"Or me." Hunter chimed in.

The paramedic gave Rebecca a paper with some general information about shock, then quickly left the apartment.

Hunter turned to Rebecca and said, "I know you'd probably like this night to be over with, but I have to take your statement. It's best to do it as soon as possible. Are you ok with that?"

"To be honest, I'd rather go ahead and get all this over with as soon as possible," Rebecca told him with a sigh. "I want to put it all behind me."

Rebecca motioned for Hunter and Kari to sit on the couch. In typical Rebecca style, she grabbed a few throw pillows hidden behind a potted plant and sat crossed legged on one of them while clutching the other.

"Why was Damon here tonight?" Hunter asked.

"I'm still a little sketchy about that myself," Rebecca stated. "He came by about an hour before you arrived and said he wanted to see some of my work. I let him in thinking that's all it was. The next thing I knew, he had a knife in his hand and was saying that he couldn't let me tell anyone his secret. Then you knocked on my door."

"What secret?" Kari asked.

"Damon was afraid that I was going to tell someone that he knew the dead woman."

Hunter and Kari both looked shocked.

"You knew Damon and the deceased were acquainted with one another?" Hunter asked incredulously. "Why didn't you report this the night of the murder?"

"Look, all I know is that Damon said he wasn't going to let me tell you that he knew her," Rebecca said, shaking her head. "But I swear to you, I don't know what he was talking about!"

Hunter was confused. "Rebecca, I don't understand. Why did Damon think you knew he and the deceased were acquainted?"

"I was in the basement doing laundry earlier today. Damon brought up the murder and I said that I thought I had seen the dead woman before. I guess he thought I was talking about seeing them together here, but I wasn't. I did a summer internship at a small theatre in Portland a while back. I think I met her while I was there."

"That would make sense," Kari said. "Ms. Moore was an actress in a theatre in Portland."

Hunter thought about her explanation for a moment, then offered, "Well, I'm glad Kari and I figured out that Damon was the killer earlier today. Otherwise, we wouldn't have been here in time."

"How did you know it was Damon?" Rebecca wanted to know.

"Now that's an odd story," Hunter told her. "Early in the investigation, we dismissed Damon as a suspect because we didn't think he was capable of climbing those stairs with crutches. However, Kari and Kasi saw him throw something in the lake today. As it turns out, it was an engagement ring meant for Kelsey Moore."

Rebecca gasped, "Oh my! I take it that she turned him down?"

"That's what I'm about to find out." Hunter turned to Kari and said, "I have to head back to the station and then go to the hospital to question Damon again. Would you like me to ask someone to take you home?"

"No need, I want to stay here with Rebecca for a while," Kari told him. "She's been through so much today."

"That's probably a good idea."

As he walked to his car, Hunter couldn't help but feel a little bummed that he wasn't going to be able to spend some more time with Kari.

But now that this case is over, maybe I'll have time to go on another date with her, he thought.

Hunter had some paperwork to complete before he headed over to the hospital. By the time he was done, though, Jo was bringing Damon through the doors of the station. He got up to see what was going on.

After she deposited Greer in an interrogation room, Hunter approached his sometimes partner. "I take it they released Greer from the hospital already?"

"Yes, unfortunately, the kick Ms. Trang gave him didn't result in any major damage," Jo said drily. "He'll be swollen for a while, but he was fit enough to be returned to the station after a very quick trip to the ER."

"Good, I was hoping we could get a crack at interrogating him today."

"Yep, I figured that you would want to have a little chat with him the moment we got back."

"Thanks, Jo." Hunter rubbed his hands back and forth as if warming them.

That old familiar feeling Hunter got every time he was about to interrogate someone slowly crept back in and he knew he was in his element.

Okay, Damon, it's time for a confession.

Chapter 24

Kari

The next morning, Kasi assured her sister that she could sleep in after her debacle at the Abbey and that she'd be happy to handle the morning rush. Kari, however, was still shaken from the run-in with Damon and didn't want to be alone.

After staying with Rebecca for a few hours the night before to ensure her friend was okay, Rebecca had taken her home and stayed for a glass of wine with her and Kasi. She listened to the details of what had happened with wide eyes, her fear for her sister's safety evident on her face.

After Rebecca had left, the sisters sat on the couch together, neither of them speaking. They finally put on a movie, but it was clear after a few minutes that they weren't even watching it. However, neither of them had been ready for bed, either.

They ended up making a pot of tea and staying up past eleven, talking about what had happened and how relieved they were that it was finally over.

"Oh look, it's the master detective," Kasi said, glancing up as the bell over the coffee shop door tinkled.

"Hello ladies!" Hunter strolled up to the counter and leaned one elbow on it. "Guess who got a full confession from Mr. Damon Greer?"

"Matlock?" Kasi tried, and Kari punched her playfully in the arm.

"What did he say?" Kari asked after ensuring that no customers were close enough to listen in on their conversation. "He really admitted to killing her?"

"Yes, indeed he did!" Hunter said proudly.

The girls waited, but Hunter didn't offer any more details.

"Spit it out, man!" Kasi cried, causing the lone customers in the corner to jump in their seats.

"Jeez, are you trying to create drama or what? Who knew you were such a diva?" Kari said with a chuckle. "Let him tell it on his own time."

"Fine," Kasi said with a big sigh, but she kept giving Hunter a look that said, *If you don't tell us what happened right now, I'm going to jump over this counter and break your legs.*

"Those caramel bars are looking mighty tasty," Hunter said, gazing at the case on the counter. "Some sugar might be just what I need to tell this story."

196

Kari grabbed Kasi's arm before her sister could make good on her implied threat. "Hunter, seriously! What did he say?"

Hunter snickered. "All right, all right. It turns out that Damon was totally in love with Kelsey. The two of them had a little fling back in Portland, but he wanted to get serious. Kelsey thought they were just having fun and didn't want anything more, but Damon kept trying to convince her they would be perfect together."

"And that caused him to murder her?" Kasi asked, aghast. "That's one way to guarantee they'd never be together!"

Hunter held up a hand. "I'm not finished. Apparently, as Damon was working on one of the set designs, he happened to see Kelsey smooching it up with one of the theater's producers. Poor ol' Damon, who'd actually bought an engagement ring for Kelsey, was so shocked that he fell off his perch and smashed his ankle."

"Ahh, so that's why he was on crutches," Kari said with a nod. "But why did he decide to come to Mills Township?"

"I think he first did it just to get some space and distance from the situation," Hunter explained. "But he just couldn't get Kelsey off his mind, so he devised a little plan to get her to come join him."

"Why would she do that?" Kasi asked. "She didn't even like the guy, apparently!"

"He made up a story about producing a historical mystery about the ghost nun," Hunter answered. "He told her he was thinking of her for the lead and that she needed to come meet him to audition for the part. When she got here, he said the audition would be to recreate the falling nun scene and that she had to drink a goblet of altar wine before going up on the roof."

"The wine was poisoned, wasn't it?" Kasi hissed. "That snake!"

"Indeed, it was," Hunter confirmed. "She was so messed up by the time she made it to the roof, it would've been a miracle if she wouldn't have fallen off."

"And no one saw him that night?" Kari asked, shocked.

"The Finches made quite a ruckus when they found her," Hunter said. "People came running when Mandy screamed, and Damon was able to just blend in with the crowd."

"Wow," Kari breathed. "I can't believe this is finally over. Maybe now the town can go back to normal."

"I wouldn't mind keeping some of our new customers," Kasi said cheekily, raising her hands when she saw her sister's glare. "What? I don't mean I want another murder; I'm just saying that the increase in tourism has been pretty nice for our bottom line."

"I'm not sure things in Mills will ever be the same again," Hunter said, his earlier good mood fading. "This was a pretty dark incident. Even though neither the killer nor the victim were locals, it will still have an impact."

"Soooo," Hunter said when Kasi had disappeared into the back room to check on a batch of scones in the oven, "what would you say to re-creating our date that this case so rudely interrupted?"

Kari heart leapt in her chest. "Hmmmm, I think that sounds like a mighty fine idea, Hunter Houston. What would you like to do?"

"I was thinking a nice dinner and maybe a stroll around town?" Hunter said. "It's supposed to be a really nice evening, and it will be nice to get out and about now that all the tourists are going back home."

"I think that sounds perfect." Kari realized that she had been craving some time alone with Hunter—time that did not include trying to identify a dead body or chasing down suspects.

"Meet you here at 6 o'clock?" At her nod, he leaned over the counter and gave her a quick peck on the cheek. "I'm not sure I thanked you for your uncanny ability to snoop, Kari. I don't think we could have solved this one without you."

"What about me?" came Kasi's holler from the back room.

Kari burst out laughing. "That girl has the ears of a bat!" she whispered.

"I heard that, too!" Kasi yelled, causing Hunter to start chuckling as well.

"Thank you, Kasi!" Hunter hollered over the counter. "Your amateur sleuthing is much appreciated!"

"You'd better watch out," Kari told him teasingly, patting his cheek. "Kasi and I might just have to shut down the coffee shop and join the police force."

"None of the guys at the station would be able to get an ounce of work done with the two of you, pretty ladies, working there," Hunter told her with a smile. "Besides, where would we get our caffeine fixes?"

"Yo, Hunter, my main man!" A blond man with a mohawk and a broad smile walked up behind Hunter and slapped him a high five. "I was just walking by when I saw you in here, and thought I'd stop in to say what's up?"

"Jake!" Hunter said, clearly happy to see the man. "I haven't seen you forever! I thought you were still on tour?" He turned to Kari. "This just happens to be one half of Mills Township's own Fire Spitters!"

"What?" Kari exclaimed. The Fire Spitters were a rap duo that had taken off in popularity in the last couple of years and happened to be one of Kari's favorite entertainers. "It's so great to meet you! I'm a huge fan!"

She giddily yelled to her sister, "Kasi! It's Jake from the Fire Spitters!"

"Cool," Kasi called back from the kitchen. She was not a huge fan, instead preferring punk rock over rap.

"Whatever you want is on the house!" Kari said, her huge grin hurting her face.

"I'd love an espresso, but I'd be happy to pay for it," Jake replied.

As Kari made the drink, the three of them chatted comfortably about Jake's recent tour, the success of the coffee shop, and the murder case they had just solved. If any of them had looked out the window, they would've seen that the danger wasn't really behind them. In fact, it was right outside their door.

Killer

The killer tried to be follow his prey without being noticed. It wasn't that hard, no one ever noticed the Killer whenever he was around. It was always about him.

I'm tired of his leftovers! The Killer thought.

A long time ago, the Killer had no ill feelings toward the victim but after years of living in his shadow, the Killer couldn't take it any longer. The admiration and respect for him had withered and died a long time ago. Now, all that was in its place was disgust.

The killer tried to calm the rage that threatened to burst forth and exact the revenge so desperately clawing its way to the surface.

Keep it together! The Killer thought. *In due time, all my patience and planning will be worth it. I'll make him pay with his life for his insolence.*

From a safe distance, the Killer managed to suppress the anger. Satisfied that it wouldn't be long before the victim was gone forever, the Killer continued to follow him.

Everywhere the victim went, people stopped and stared. Some even asked for his autograph. As always, people couldn't get enough of him.

It was no surprise to the Killer when Hunter Houston and his friend Kari stopped to talk to the victim. Like everyone else in town, they were enamored of him. *I'm sure they'll be devastated when he's dead.*

Mills Township had a lot of tragedies lately, this murder will just be another in a growing line of untimely deaths. If the Killer was lucky no one would even suspect him of the murder. And even if they did, there was no way anyone would be able to prove it.

I'm smarter than all of them, especially Houston and his nosey girlfriend! Not that it really mattered, killing two more people wouldn't be that hard.

As the victim, Hunter and Kari made their way down the street, the Killer continued to follow them.

With each star struck person the Killer silently watched fawn over the victim, the desire for revenge grew stronger.

Everyone thinks he's so special! The killer thought. *It won't be long now, and I'll be rid of him forever. Then everyone will finally see me!*

Patiently waiting and watching for the right time to make their move, the Killer has had plenty of time to make plans. The victim will never see it coming, he doesn't even realize how much the Killer hates him.

The Killer chuckled. *All these years, he's lived in the spotlight. Just wait until he realizes what I have in store for him! He's going to die all alone.*

The killer watched the group a little longer, reveling in the fact that they've gone unnoticed.

Some cop Houston is, he doesn't even realize when he's being followed. It won't be hard fooling him. They'll never suspect me!

Hearing the laughter from the victim and his friends, the Killer paused and whispered, "Enjoy your time while you have it, friends. It won't be long before I come for you!"

Thank you for reading!

© Sara Bourgeois 2019

Made in the USA
Coppell, TX
17 October 2021

64226411R00121